THE
CRUX

THE
CRUX

Lendaw Series: Book 1

R. J. CONFIANT

Copyright © 2015 by R. J. Confiant.

ISBN: Softcover   978-1-5144-0866-7
          eBook   978-1-5144-0867-4

All rights reserved. No part of this book may be reproduced or transmitted in any form or by any means, electronic or mechanical, including photocopying, recording, or by any information storage and retrieval system, without permission in writing from the copyright owner.

This is a work of fiction. Names, characters, places and incidents either are the product of the author's imagination or are used fictitiously, and any resemblance to any actual persons, living or dead, events, or locales is entirely coincidental.

Any people depicted in stock imagery provided by Thinkstock are models, and such images are being used for illustrative purposes only.
Certain stock imagery © Thinkstock.

Print information available on the last page.

Rev. date: 12/21/2015

To order additional copies of this book, contact:
Xlibris
1-888-795-4274
www.Xlibris.com
Orders@Xlibris.com
724014

CONTENTS

Acknowledgements ix
Prologue xi
Chapter 1   Revelation 1
Chapter 2   Alyra 10
Chapter 3   Serpent in our Mist 19
Chapter 4   Craft 23
Chapter 5   The Hop and Trail 28
Chapter 6   Of Age 32
Chapter 7   The Dream 40
Chapter 8   Cocidius 46
Chapter 9   Loren 51
Chapter 10   Mudluck 56
Chapter 11   Meglog 60
Chapter 12   Lost 64
Chapter 13   Muwtag 68
Chapter 14   Survivors 74
Chapter 15   MarGraven 80
Chapter 16   Escape 86
Chapter 17   Erenhil 90
Chapter 18   Skirmishes 94
Chapter 19   Reckonings 98
Chapter 20   Unexpected 103
Chapter 21   Schemes 109
Chapter 22   To War 113
Chapter 23   Old Man 117
Chapter 24   Battle of Kregen 121
Chapter 25   More Death 125
Chapter 26   Standing Ground 129

Chapter 27 An Old Foe 132
Chapter 28 Destiny 135
Chapter 29 Completions 138
Chapter 30 Aftermath 142
Chapter 31 Sad Celebrations 145
Chapter 32 Departures 149

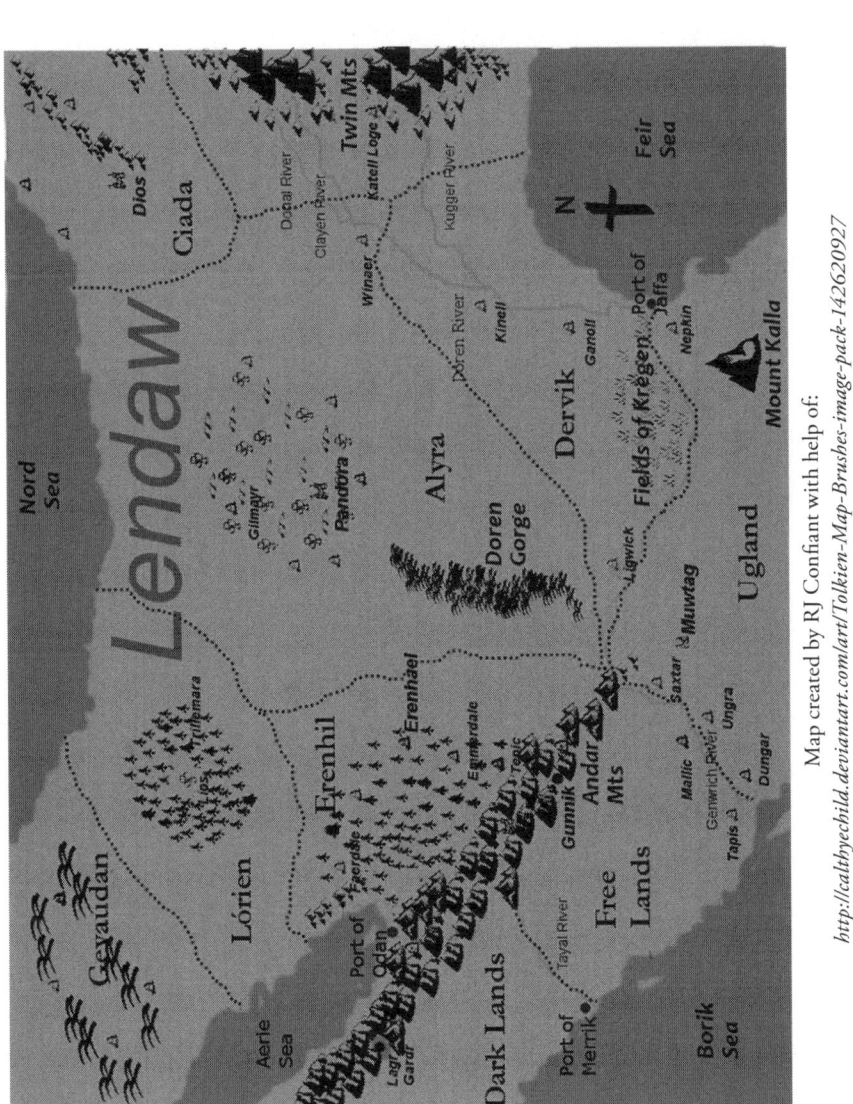

Map created by RJ Confant with help of:

http://caltbyechild.deviantart.com/art/Tolkien-Map-Brushes-image-pack-142620927
http://caltbyechild.deviantart.com/art/More-Mountains-image-pack-142620631
http://thewhitecrayon.deviantart.com/art/TSMB-The-GIMP-Edition-151774168

Acknowledgements

I would like to express my appreciation for all those who supported me during the writing of this book; to all those who read, wrote or offered comments. I especially like to thank those who assisted in the editing, proofreading and design of this book.

I would like to recognize all those at Xlibris Self-Publishing, especially Dana Goulding and Charles Freemont, for assisting me to publish this book.

I thank my partner Douglas Carlson for his support and patience through the long and difficult process of publishing this book.

Thanks to Lee Nicholson for being my primary reader and Iain Jamison. I greatly appreciate all their input and advice during the writing of this book.

Finally, no one person really completes a task alone. I ask for understanding of those whose names I failed to mention and yet who have been a great support to me over the years. To all my family and all my friends I say, "Thank-you."

Prologue

The dog sat atop the hill and looked down into the vale. To an observer below, it appeared as if the dog was studying its surroundings, which of course it was as this was no ordinary dog. His name was Alistair and he was a Morphan, a change shifter, a person who could transform into other creatures. Alistair was a powerful wizard. In his usual form, Alistair stood six feet and six inches. He had long, wavy white hair and beard, which hung down, past his chest. His skin was smooth with only a few wrinkles around the eyes and around the mouth when he smiled. His eyes were a mixture of blue and green that stared with such piercing intensity they made one squirm uncomfortably. On first impression, he came across as quite serious and straightforward, which he was to a point. Alistair was likewise very personable, friendly, and jovial.

Alistair was on a planet called Terra. The people of the world called it "Earth". Instead of magic, these people practiced science. *This world has changed greatly since the last time I visited. I am somewhat awed at what I see: giant machines, vehicles, buildings and cities span the planet. I guess it was foolish of me to hope things would remain the same. The last time I was here was a thousand years ago.* He shook his head and chuckled to himself. *Change was bound to happen, it always does. The world turns and time goes on. It is the nature of things.*

Alistair was from a world called Lendaw, a planet on the cusp of war, a war that would destroy his world, as he knew it. Already the dark forces were rising. For a long time, Anko lay dormant until recently. Now there were signs of his return. Already Anko's forces gathered at the fields of Kregen - trolls, giants, ogres, wizards, witches and shades, while his henchmen Donar, Keric, and Nivel were in hot pursuit, and not very far behind Alistair himself. His last hope for salvation laid in locating a girl. Alistair was on Earth because of a prophecy:

> "One will come who will be of, but not from Lendaw. One who will have the power that Anko cannot defeat. With the finding of the one, Anko's domain will cease to be forever."

On his hunt to find the person of whom the prophecy spoke, Alistair travelled to many worlds and to different eras. All with the same result, the trail always returned to the girl. In discovering the girl, Alistair believed he likewise found the fulfillment of said prophecy.

Alistair never expected to find the one in such a humble abode. He knew from experience that sometimes greatness comes from humble beginnings. He himself was proof.

An eon ago, he learnt that he was a wizard and that he apprenticed with the High Wizard Nairn who took him in. At first Alistair thought, Nairn made an error. After all, how could he become a wizard because he showed no outward signs of being one? He showed no signs at all.

Alistair came from a poor family in the town of Mallic on the outskirts of the Free Lands a country of nomadic and tribal people. Life in Mallic was not always easy. Most of the time he struggled to make a living. On many occasions, he had to beg off the kindness of strangers. He had no father. His mother worked and cared for the family. He was the eldest of five children, and as such, he left school as soon as possible to help with the family. Since he was the eldest and a son, he felt obligated to work and to earn a living to feed and clothe the rest of his siblings. Despite the fact that life was difficult, it was a happy existence.

When Nairn asked first his mother if he could take Alistair as his apprentice, Alistair's mother, Kendra, was hesitant. Alistair was her eldest son, and as such, she required what little money he brought in to help sustain the family. Alistair's sister, Hanna, ensured their mother she was able to take his place as the main breadwinner and utterly capable of helping care for the family. After much debate, Kendra relented and she allowed Alistair to leave. She released Alistair to Nairn's care. To ease the loss of Alistair, Nairn gave Kendra one hundred Pistole. Alistair packed what few possessions he had, said good-bye to his family and left with Nairn. He was never to see his family again.

Alistair was about to do the same. History was about to repeat itself. He was about to take Jenna from the only family she knew.

CHAPTER 1

Revelation

As Alistair stared out across the span, he pondered as to what his next move should be. He took out the Gaper, looked over its glossy, smooth surface, and concentrated on the girl. Immediately the image of the girl appeared on the surface and in the background, he noted the name of a school: "Darmouth High School."

As good as any place to start.

Melville was a small mid-western city with a population of about seven thousand and five hundred people. Once just a farming community, now a growing metropolis with its success founded on farming grains, and mining potash and uranium. Alastair walked along the sidewalk of Main Street where two and three story red-bricked buildings lined the street hinting at the city's earlier days. Off the Main Street, Alistair observed newer small to mid-size buildings that sprouted up, a clue to the city's modern times. Distracted by the wonder of it all, Alastair literally bumped into a woman on the sidewalk. Alastair caught her before she fell. Alastair smiled and apologized. He asked the woman for directions to Darmouth High School. She smiled and she gave him the directions he required. It was a half hour before he reached his destination. Alistair transformed into a dog as he neared his destination. He sat and observed. After a few hours of observation, he spotted Jenna easily enough.

Her elven features exposed her as non-human. She was very tall and lean almost to the point of being anorexic. Her face was thin with angular features and her eyebrows arched upward ever so slightly. She had green eyes and she wore glasses. Her hair was shiny red and long as to fall to her lower back. Alistair was sure that her hair concealed the pointy and protruding ears common to Elvenkind. Alistair was unsure of the reason for her concealment. *Perhaps she is ashamed of them or perhaps, she simply wished to hide the fact that she was not quite human.* Either way, it was obvious to him that the girl was not of this Earth.

Jenna considered herself quite the tomboy. She even dressed the part. Her usual attire consisted of a shirt, pants and runners. Thus, when Alistair first saw her he thought she was wearing riding attire.

Alistair estimated her age to be sixteen years. *She was too old to be an apprentice. A pity, as he did not currently have one. The position was currently vacant.*

He followed her throughout the next few days. He noticed Jenna possessed few friends, two or three, that he could observe. She appeared very relaxed and more joyful when she was with them.

When not with friends, Jenna sat alone at one of the benches, or she sat under a tree studying one of the many books in her possession.

It appeared, to him, that Jenna had a strong desire to learn. He found this an honorable trait. Jenna was what many, at her school considered a 'geek.' Perhaps some people would consider such thought snobbish. Jenna, herself, appeared to wear the title with pride.

Alistair desperately needed to extract the girl. He knew this would be difficult, if not impossible to accomplish. Alistair had to be careful and he was unsure how to proceed. In his world, retrieving the girl was a simple process of asking her guardian for permission. The process was more complication on Terra. The Terrans, as he knew Earth inhabitants, had authorities known as "police." He did not wish the police to arrest him in his attempt to acquire the girl. In addition, Jenna could show resistance. He was after all a complete stranger to her.

He shrugged his shoulders.

There had to be a way to make this happen. He needed to proceed cautiously.

Now, how can I approach the girl without scaring her away?

An idea popped into his head and without any further delay, Alistair transformed himself into a dog.

Alistair trailed Jenna for four days. It was then that he decided to make his move. He strode over to Jenna and then he paused. Jenna noticed the dog and called it over. Alistair obeyed. He approached cautiously wagging his tail. Jenna reached down and patted the dog on the head, "What a cute doggy you are! Who's a good boy then?" Alistair grabbed Jenna's scent thinking he would be able to trail her should he lose her sight. Alistair barked and strode away.

Later, Alistair followed Jenna to her farmhouse located near Seventh Avenue on the outskirts of a small town called Melville, which was smack dab in the middle of nowhere, or so it seemed. As Jenna opened the door to her home, Dot greeted her. Jenna closed the door behind her and she returned the greeting.

Alistair watched from a distance.

The house was old and it begun to show signs of wear and tear. There were boards missing on the white picket fence, and the paint cracked and peeled on the remaining boards. Some of the tiles on the roof were moldy and they had moss growing around their edges. A few tiles were broken and the odd one went missing. The uncut grass and the over grown weeds proved the yard was un-kept. The house was very modest.

Jenna lived with her adoptive parents Dot and Matt who worked long hours to earn a meagerly wage, while Jenna attended school during the day. She spent her evenings studying until late in the night. Jenna worked one night a week and one day on the weekend to earn enough for school supplies, and some pocket money. She considered herself an unpretentious girl. She rarely wore dresses, nor did she bother with make-up, except on special occasions and usually with great discomfort. Jenna was smart. She would help anyone who asked. Although her life was modest, Jenna did not want. She had everything she needed. She had a happy and loving home. Jenna was content.

Thunder roared in the distance and an eerie light flashed across the evening sky. Alistair looked up.

Something is wrong.

It took a moment for Alistair spot it. The beast was huge, as tall as a ten-story building. The Gargon gave a great roar. It was black; blacker than anything Alistair had ever seen before and the creature seemed a warped version of its brothers and sisters the dragons. It was two-headed, its scales seemed like armored plating, its mouths were round in shape and it had multi-layered shark-like teeth.

Mounted upon its back was Donar, a Shadeen: A black wraith-like creature, once a magician like Alastair. Donar practiced the dark arts and overtime they corrupted him. Their power wore at him until he was, but a shadow of his former self, and enslaved to Anko his lord and master. Donar was one of seven such creatures known to exist.

Were there others? Have they come into this world as well? I must be careful.

Alistair needed to act quickly. He transformed back to his natural form of a man, he cursed and ran for the door of the house banged on the door and shouted, "Get out! Get out quickly. I have put you all in danger. Come quickly."

Panic-stricken Jenna opened the door and rushed out, closely followed by Dot and Matt. Looking up in the sky, Dot let out a scream.

Alistair shouted, "My name is Alistair and I mean you no harm. Do you believe me?"

Too frightened to respond, they stood there dumbstruck.

Alistair continued, "If you wish to survive, you must listen and do as I say!"

Speechlessly, they nodded.

"Tego texi tectum maximus," mumbled Alistair, with his arms stretching over Jenna, Dot and Matt. At once, a great, glowing shield immediately surrounded the three of them.

"Whatever happens, don't move and stay here," ordered Alistair. He turned his attention to Donar. "Donar, you should not have come this far from your home. You do not belong in this world".

Donar gave a sinister laugh. "I do not fear you, Alistair," Donar sneered.

The two faced each other to do battle.

As Donar descended towards him, Alistair stood his ground and he raised his staff high and yelled, "Interficio!" The force of the spell hit the gargon's breastplate and it stumbled backward before it regained its bearing and it halted in mid-air. Donar clung to hang on.

Donar raised his staff and he responded with his own spell.

Alistair swerved and quickly raised a protective shield.

The battle raged onward. Alistair and Donar alternated between attacks; one upon the other, each opponent used all the force that he could muster to attack his opponent. Alistair staggered backward with each strike of magic.

All at once, Keric, Nivel and their men appeared from behind. Alistair began to despair. With the others involved, Alistair had no chance of winning this fight.

Moreover, to make things worse witnessed Jenna entering the battlefield. Panic overcame him.

What is she doing?

Jenna stood and watched from behind the protective shield, she knew that Alistair was faltering and that defeat was inevitable. She knew she had to do something. She realized that she could not stand by and do nothing, while Alistair battled to protect her and her family.

Then the strangest thing happened. As if by some bizarre flash of clarity, she suddenly and intuitively knew exactly what to do. It was as if somebody, or something, guiding her thoughts and her movements, Jenna stepped out from the protection of the shield. Calmly she walked towards the flying beast. She reached into her shirt and grasped the chain that hung around her neck she pulled it out and held it aloft she yelled, "STOP!"

Many things occurred at once, attached to the chain was a stone. It exploded with the brightest light she had ever seen. The power from the stone shot out in all directions. Firstly, it struck Donar and the gargon, followed by Keric, Nivel and their herdsmen. The power from the stone grew with greater intensity. Jenna was terrified. To conceal her fear, she kept her hand on the stone.

The wind gathered strength. It swirled and it swooshed in all directions and soon it formed a whirlpool. The eddy surrounded the gargon and the strange men, and then the sky opened. The funnel, for that was what it now was, lifted the attackers from their current positions and flung them, like rag dolls, into the rift. Once they went through the passage, the rift quickly sealed itself.

Alistair sank to the ground exhausted. He turned toward Jenna, he sighed with relief, and he whispered, "You can let go now, my dear."

Jenna released the stone.

"What happened?" Jenna asked.

Alistair laughed. "It's a long story, my dear girl," he said. "Shall we gather your parents and go into the house?" He rose and walked with Jenna toward her parents and hurried them all into the house. Once in the sitting room, Jenna, Dot and Matt stared at Alistair as he closed all the doors and drew the curtains. There was a chill in the air. He looked at the fireplace, and muttered the word "Aduro" to which the fireplace lit up with a cozy, warm fire.

"I have important information to convey with you. Will you hear me out completely and then you can either ask me to leave or let me stay a while?"

The three Earthlings looked at each other and collectively turned back to Alistair and nodded. They were speechless.

"Well, for the first time in a long time, I don't know where to begin," stated a perplexed Alistair. He paced up and down in front of the fireplace gathering his thoughts, his body casting flickering shadows against the wall. Then he began to speak, "I have told you my name and nothing else. Now for the difficult part, I omitted where I come from. I am not from this world. My world is Lendaw, which is quite different from yours. In your world, you have science. In mine, we practice magic. As you have seen, I am a wizard. I am also a change shifter. I can change into whatever I want even a dog." Jenna turned to Alistair realizing that they had already met once today. "Yes, that's right. I was following you. You see it was my duty to find you and to protect you. In my haste to find you, I have inadvertently brought danger to you and your parents."

He turned to the Humes, "I know these two are not your real parents. I knew your father Turwyn and he is not an Earthling. You are Jenna heir to Queen Maia. You are both part Terran and Lendawan." Jenna was shocked! She was about to speak when Alistair held her off.

Time on Earth is slower than that of Lendaw. By your reckoning, Turwyn arrived on Earth two decades ago. During that period, Lendaw experienced two centuries since time on Lendaw moves much faster than Earth.

Turwyn came to Earth because your lineage is Lendaw's only hope. The Council decided that your father needed to leave Lendaw. The question was where to go and Terra, what you call 'Earth', was the most logical choice: Firstly, from Lendaw's point of view, Terra is young. Secondly, the planet practices science and not magic, thus it posed no threat to Lendaw and lastly, humankind is a unique species. It is unlike any other species in the universe. Humankind has the capacity for such great love and much hatred, to condemn and yet to forgive, to destroy and yet to inspire change. Yours is a species of contradictions. These are great traits and they not so easily to found in many races. Your traits are not the only thing that set your people apart.

Terrans have un-quenching thirst for knowledge, a conceit in yourselves and a belief that humanity can accomplish anything it sets its mind to. I have never seen so many traits in one race and to such intensity.

Everyone was silent for quite a few minutes.

Finally Jenna spoke, "This has got to be a joke. Surely you are joking?"

Alistair responded, "It's hard to believe. I know. The truth can be difficult to hear. Turwyn would have told you the truth when you came of age. His premature death prevented him from telling you."

Looking at the Humes, Alistair stated, "It is time for you two to share your story."

Dot looked at Matt, and Matt looked over to Dot both were silent until Dot nodded to Matt. Matt took control, and looking at Jenna, he started his tale.

We knew your parents Michael and Patricia MacDougall. When we met them, you were just two years old. To us they seemed like any other couple. Shortly after your fourth birthday, we received bad news. A police officer showed up at the door. He informed us that your father and mother died in a car crash. Eventually, we got custody of you. As we were unable to have our own children, we were happy to oblige.

One day, a number of years later, Dot was going through your parents' things and she happened upon a letter, hitherto over looked. The letter it explained everything. It explained that your father was Lendawan and that he settled on Earth taking on the name of Patrick MacDougall. It continued that he met your mother, fell in love, wed, and gave birth to you.

After reading the letter, we did not believe it. It seemed impossible. Over time, we came to believe. While you were young, you orchestrated many strange feats. At first, we brushed them off as coincidences or happenstance. Later, these occurrences grew more outrageous until we could no longer deny their existence.

We found a gemstone. With it, Dot fashioned the amulet you wear around your neck.

Matt stopped and he surveyed Dot.

No one said a word.

Finally, Alistair asked, "Now, about that stone. May I examine it?" Jenna showed Alistair the broach. It gleamed in the light. It was blue of a shade not found on Earth. 'It was Einn Stone: a tool of the Light handed down from the Pantheon to the House of Weir", explained Alistair. "What do you remember of your parents?"

Jenna paused for a moment, she had not thought of them in a long time.

"I can remember only fragments. They are more images than words", replied Jenna.

"Turwyn was of noble birth and a great wizard in his own right. He fought in the Battle of Ugland. Where Turwyn used the Iluminar to defeated Anko, the under-lord of Urian, and shattered the Gentra: The Crystal of Power. The blast from the explosion injured Anko where he laid comatose. As he lay dormant, the Uglandan went into hiding. Now, he is conscious and his followers have returned. With each passing day, Anko's health strengthens. The Uglandan become more brazen. They terrorize neighboring towns and murder indiscriminately. Their objective is to spread fear wherever they go."

Alistair stared at Jenna and stated simply, "I need you to come back with me to Lendaw!"

"Me!" replied a shocked Jenna. "What could you possibly want with me?"

"I believe that you are the one I have been searching for, and after the attack by the Uglandan today, there can be no further doubt. It is sufficient to say, 'you are needed.' In any event, you can no longer remain here. The Uglandan will return and they will return in greater numbers. It is no longer safe for either you or your family. You and the Humes both need to leave and soon!"

Silence filled the room. Jenna feared the loss of all that she ever had. The Humes were the only family Jenna truly really knew. Jenna did not wish to depart from them.

Finally, Dot spoke for them, "It is decided then. We shall leave. Matt and I will go into hiding. Jenna you must go with Alistair. There is no time to waste. We are all in danger if we stay. We will require a ruse. Perhaps we die in a fire or an accident. It really does not matter which one. We require anything that will mask our true intent of escape. Alistair, I believe, you can help with this. Matt and I will head to Latin America and open up that restaurant we always wanted. We will need to use aliases and to borrow some the funds from Jenna's inheritance."

Jenna listened to all of this in disbelief. She could not believe anything she heard.

It took four days to get everything ready for their departure. The Humes went to the bank and arranged an account for Jenna should she require one in the future. They opened offshore accounts in various countries and transferred funds into each one. They arranged management of the manor that Jenna would one day inherit.

Jenna went to pack her backpack with a few of her belongings. The Humes meanwhile went to their room and packed two suitcases and a carry-on bag.

When all was ready, they gathered in the living room to finalize the plan.

Alistair planned the idea of an accidental gas explosion in the house. The explosion would occur at dusk. It would seem of if they were all home at suppertime when the calamity occurred, and that they had all perished in the explosion. Just prior to the mishap, Alistair would transfer them to a spot on the outskirts of Melville. From there, they would say their goodbyes and go their separate ways.

As dusk approached, they gathered at the rendezvous point. While Jenna and the Humes bid their farewells, Alistair returned to set the house and with a whisper sent the house ablaze with a huge explosion. He transformed into a dog and walked away. The plan had worked perfectly!

CHAPTER 2

Alyra

The mist rose over the Alyran plains with an irritable frequency. The group had been travelling for almost nine pace-stays. For the last five of these pace-stays, the dwarves had endured constant rainfall. Durkin was sick of it. He was grumpy. Grumpier than he normally was and he voiced his displeasure with every turn on the road. After a while, Durkin snapped at anyone attempted to mollify him. Finally, Bilpin could take no more. "Take it easy Durkin, we'll be there after nightfall," retorted Bilpin, "We only need to exit this valley."

The dwarves proceeded onward to Pandora, the capital of Alyra a country situated in the central Lendaw. Durkin reflected on how never cared for Pandora with its green lands and rolling hills. He preferred his own home located in the center of the Andar Mountains. Gunnik was the biggest and the best of all the dwarf settlements. Most dwarves considered Gunnik to be the "Jewel of the South." The settlement took two centuries to fashion into its current form. It was the pride of the dwarves and the source of their strength.

From the western region of Lendaw, another group travelled to Alyra. Danyll rode on horseback beside Cryall his sister. He voiced his opinions and speculations as to the possible reasons for their journey. Cryall listened silently with little response. She knew he did not know the reason for the journey any more than she did. All they knew was that they were requested accompany the royal party and to provide security if it was deemed necessary. Danyll and Cryall were excellent archers. They were well proficient in the art of warfare. The elves would arrive by nightfall and Cryall was glad for she needed the break.

Jenna had arrived in Pandora two days prior to the arrival of the elves and dwarves. From the moment she arrived on Lendaw, Jenna knew she was on a different world. Lendaw had two stars and three moons. The sky was pinkish in color. Jenna was awed by this sight and she explained to Alistair that it reminded her of pictures she saw on Earth's neighboring planet Mars. The plant life on Lendaw was similar to that of Earth with some exceptions. Upon further observation, Jenna saw that there were some strange plants as well. Alistair told her that he would one day teach her about them. Some plants were safe to touch and eat while other plants were extremely dangerous. He advised her to ask about any plant before she ate or touch any of them.

The trip from the Portal of Ianua, located within the Twin Mountains region of Lendaw, took three and a half pace-stays, or a little less than three and a half days, as Alistair explained. Alistair described the geography of Lendaw and some of its history as they walked to the capital of Pandora. The primary races were elves, dwarves, men, gnomes, trolls, giants, and ogres. Jenna learnt that there were Shadeen, wizards, witches and seers.

After the first day of their journey, Jenna discovered that she no longer required her glasses. She took them off, placed them in the case, and shoved them in her knapsack. Alistair surmised that differences between Earth and Lendaw's atmospheric composition, and Jenna's genetic predisposition made it necessary for glasses on Earth and that she no longer required them now that she was on Lendaw.

The duo reached the outskirts of the city.

Up ahead, Jenna spotted a guard approach on horseback. The guard dismounted and she approached Alistair. She spoke with him briefly. He whispered something Jenna was unable to hear. The guard looked at Jenna and she bowed slightly. The officer then climbed her horse and drove away. Alistair turned to Jenna and he stated, "The Council requests our presence."

The two passed through the city streets. Jenna noticed that its occupants meek and hardworking people. The people what they were doing and peered at them as Jenna and Alistair ascended the roadway toward the castle.

The castle was gigantic. Jenna had never seen the likes it. Jenna had an inkling it was immensely old, yet showed very little wear, or decay. The walls were smooth as glass and made of greyish-black stone. The bridge across the moat spanned twenty feet high and ten feet wide. The gateway to the courtyard was forty feet in height. The courtyard was full of activity until Jenna came into view at which point most people paused what they were doing to witness the stranger passing through.

A lone woman greeted Alistair and Jenna at the doors to the castle. The woman bowed to both of them and she greeted them paying particular attention to Jenna. "Excuse me for staring… a-a-h-h", she paused. Alistair replied, "Jenna, her name is Jenna." He continued, "Jenna, this is Lady Hamilton." Lady Hamilton smiled humorously, "You look so much like your father." She took Jenna's arm. She led Jenna down the hallway. Lady Hamilton said, "We must get you to your appointed chamber and change your clothes before we head to the council chamber. It would not do well to go before the Council in your current attire. Alistair, we take your leave. I will see to Jenna's care."

Lady Hamilton escorted Jenna to her assigned chambers. Alastair watched slightly amused as Jenna turned her head back with an expression of dread. Alastair turned around and headed in the opposite direction toward the Council chambers.

"My Lords," said Alistair as he settled in front of the Council. "Ah, Alistair," replied Donyld. "We were just discussing the latest news. Since you have been absent, perhaps you are unaware of current events. Our scouts, Davin and Lowrek, disappeared a month ago. They left to discover whether the rumors of activity at Mount Kalla were true. When they did not return, we sent a search party of ten to seek hunt for them. Alas, only one of them returned and she was badly injured. We doubt she will survive to explain what occurred. We do not wish to send further troops until we can determine what has happened in Ugland." Alistair replied, "I may be able to shed some light on current events." Alistair reported to the Council all that had occurred on his trip to Terra, namely, the appearances of Donar and the Gargon, Keric and Nivel, and Jenna's arrival to Lendaw. "It appears that Anko's forces are once again on the offensive. The question is why?"

"Unknown, we requested an assembly. The dwarves, elves and the other races were invited. Only the dwarves and the elves accepted our invitation. They will arrive in a pace-stay or two. Perhaps it is best we disperse and reconvene at that time. As the others left the chamber, Alistair pulled Donyld aside and whispered, "We have been betrayed. Anko's forces knew where I was and what I was doing." Donyld frowned, "It seems highly unlikely that Donar, Keric and Nivel were there by chance. We must keep vigilant and stay alert for any clue that could help us expose the culprit. In the meantime, we shall see to Jenna care."

Lady Hamilton was at a loss by the time Alistair and Donyld arrived. The girl absolutely refused to wear anything set for her. Jenna spied the gowns and dresses laid out upon the wardrobe, "Is this what I am expected to wear?"

"This is what is expected of any lady while at the castle," replied a perplexed Lady Hamilton as she held up a dress for inspection.

Jenna lost it, "I will not wear that dress or any other. I don't wear dresses in my own world and I will not start wearing them while I am visiting Lendaw."

After the two debated, Jenna settled on pants and a shirt that Cáel, Lord Donyld's son, supplied her. Donyld entered the room and he noticed Jenna and he jokingly replied, "Nice outfit."

Jenna turned and noticed Alistair. She sighed and smiled.

"Jenna, this is Lord Donyld, speaker of the Council and my friend. Donyld, meet Jenna of the Weir," Jenna held out her hand to shake.

Donyld looked at her extended hand with confusion. An instant later, instead he bowed and stated, "My lady. I hope all is well. It has been a long time since your kindred resided in Pandora. Welcome back, I hope you will find your stay pleasant."

Donyld nodded to Lady Hamilton with courteousness and continued, "I heard you've had some excitement; Alistair has filled me in. Let us walk." Jenna, Alistair and Donyld left the chambers and they walked down the corridor.

Donyld explained to Jenna about the search party. Like Alistair, he believed Jenna played a pivotal role in this saga.

Donyld was an elf and human hybrid. His father was an elf while his mother was human. When he was younger, he lived with the elves. Later, when his mother became a member of the Council he lived with her. He became Speaker upon her death ten years past.

Jenna walked with the men as they discussed the recent events. They explained to her that the dwarves and the elves would arrive in two days. In the meantime, she was to make herself at home as much as possible. Given the strange circumstances in which she found herself, Jenna believed that relaxation would be difficult.

The next day Jenna met Cáel who was very cordial and polite.

After a few arcs, boredom set in. He offered to teach Jenna the basics of horseback riding, and defensive techniques. In such a few hours, Jenna was amazed at what she accomplished in such a short time.

If you had told her weeks ago that she would be training for battle, she would have told you were crazy. Sure Jenna was always monkeying about when she was younger still she was far from athletic. She never even considered the possibility of being an athlete. Here on Lendaw, she was surefooted and skillful. She attributed this to Cáel's encouragement and patience and nothing more.

He taught her how to play an intriguing game called Kinknox. The game was, to Jenna mind, a combination of the strategy games of chess and risk. She found the game both enjoyable and challenging. With Jenna, Cáel discovered a worthy competitor.

On the second day, while Jenna sparred with Cáel, she heard a commotion that caused her to lose concentration. Jenna turned to face the clamor. What she saw astounded her. A dozen mid-sized, men-like people, some with beards, others clean-shaven, some chubby, some lean, all dressed similarly with a cap on the head, shirts and tunics, pants and boots.

Behind the dwarves, she saw their opposite. They all appeared similar in appearance to Donyld and herself. The men and women were tall, slim and agile. The elves had angular faces, with pointy ears and golden eyes with their eyebrows flowing upwards. They all wore light clothing of shirts, pants, boots and capes except for one. The Lady, for she was truly regal Jenny could see that, wore a long green dress and cape. Beside her rode her escorts. Jenny surmised that the dwarves and elves had arrived. After they entered the courtyard, both parties halted their march and the elves dismounted.

A moment later, a party of delegates from the castle appeared and from the mix, Donyld stepped forward. Donyld spoke a greeting to all welcoming them in the ancient language, "Sal Tel Doe e Paevast."

Afterwards, he faced the dwarves, Donyld bowed. "Where is King Tharin? Who speaks in his stead?"

"I, Neofin the Quartermaster, do speak. The King sends his regrets. He could not personally attend. A matter of considerable importance required his immediate attention, a matter of which I can only discuss in the Council's chambers."

"I understand," replied Donyld.

He turned his attention to the Queen of the Elves, Donyld bowed. "Your Highness, you are most welcome."

"We thank-you, please let us dispense with the formalities and let us get down to business. In these moments, time is of the essence. Will you please escort us up into the castle?"

"As you wish Your Highness," stated Donyld.

The large group strode up toward the castle. Donyld spied Jenna and Cáel, and he turned to them, "You two should follow."

As the company continued onward, Jenna quickly caught up with Alistair who leaned over to Jenna and quietly explained it was customary, in Alyra, that the visiting Regal chair all meetings as Alyra itself no longer had one of its own.

Once inside the castle, Queen Maia turned to the elves said, "Danyll, Cryall and Tamael come with me. The rest of you see to the horses and then wait for me in my quarters."

At the same time, Neofin turned to the dwarves and told Durkin, Bilpin and a selected few to follow him. The rest he instructed to meet in his chambers.

The Council chamber was already half-full when the party arrived. Upon seeing the Queen, the crowd rose. The Queen raised her hand in protest and spoke, "Time is short. We have a feeling much has happened since we journeyed here."

The Queen spotted her usual chair, went over, and sat down. Once seated, the others followed suit and the chamber doors were sealed.

"Quartermaster we shall start with you. What has happened that the King should not show?" asked Maia.

"My Lords and Ladies", replied Neofin, "there have been numerous raids to our supplies on our eastern borders. We do not know who is behind the raids, nor the reason behind them. The culprit left few clues. We know only that our supplies have gone missing. The King has sent troops to investigate the surrounding hillsides." When he finished reporting Neofin sat down.

Donyld stood up next and recounted all that had happened in the last few quinti, or weeks, about the possible return of Anko, his re-awakening, and the troop deployment in the southeast. The Council room murmured with many voices at the announcement Anko's possible return. Maia raised her hand to silence the crowd, and stated that at this time Anko's return was only conjecture on their part. She enquired whether Donyld had anything further to report. Donyld indicated that he did not have anything else to report.

Turning to Alistair, Maia stated, "Alistair, I see you have returned. Were you successful on your mission?"

Alistair stood up addressed the room, "I believe so." He recapped the information he had provided earlier to the Council. He went on to stress the point that Anko's men seemed to know information and be in places that they should not have access to, namely, Alistair's whereabouts on Terra. Alistair then introduced Jenna to the Council. Jenna, who was not used to being the center of attention, began to squirm in her seat as all eyes set upon her. Seeing Jenna's discomfort, the Queen beckoned Jenna to sit next to her. After Jenna re-seated herself, the Queen leaned over and whispered, "You have nothing to fear for you are always welcome in my company."

"Donyld, as Speaker, do you have anything else to add?"

Donyld stood and he replied. "Only that the gnomes and the other minor races were invited to attend this meeting and they all declined our invitation. They repeated their desire to remain neutral."

"I see," she paused before continuing, "The troop movement in the south is evident though it is not the irrefutable proof. We cannot know the exact nature of the threat, if any, without further facts. Any speculation of Anko's return is just that, speculation. It may be that Anko is involved or it may not be. It could be anyone of a number of people. It could be Donar for instance. We must determine the truth. We must discover the reason behind the missing Alyrans, and the dwarf supplies only then we will have our answers. Perhaps these events are related; perhaps they are."

She observed the members around the room.

After a while, Maia addressed the weary group, "We are all tired. Let us adjourn this meeting and reconvene tomorrow."

Everyone rose.

The Queen took hold of Jenna's arm saying, "While I am here, you must stay with me. There is much to discuss and I fear we have little time." Jenna and the Queen left the chamber followed by the elves, the dwarves, Donyld with Cáel, Alistair and the rest of the group.

Maia and Jenna arrived at the Queen's appointed chambers. The room was the grandest thing Jenna had ever seen. Jenna wandered down the aisle, she looked into each room they passed, and she noticed that each room served a unique purpose. After a while, Maia sat in a chair.

"These are my private chambers. Please sit." Maia indicated to the seat beside her.

Jenna did as she asked. She walked over and sat down.

"I have to tell you, you look so much like your father. Yes, I knew Turwyn. He and I grew up together for a few years. At that time, we were best friends."

Maia laughed, "That was a lifetime ago."

The Queen grew serious again and she enquired, "So, how are you holding up? Do you have any questions, or concerns that you would like answered?" She continued, "I am not sure if I will be able to answer them all. I shall try."

"Frankly, I don't even know where to begin," sighed a frustrated Jenna and she threw up her arms, "I mean a few days ago I was just plain Jenna. I went to school, I came home, I did homework, I worked a few days a week, and I hung out with my family and friends. Now, my understanding of the world as I knew it is no more. I have lost my family, I had strange creatures try to kill me, I met a man who can change into a dog, and I discovered that wizards, dragon, dwarves and elves are all real! I don't know what I am doing here. I do not belong in this world. This world is strange to me. I might as well be in King Arthur's court. That's it, that's what this world reminds me of a fairy tale."

Maia looked at Jenna with sympathy and sighed, "I am afraid the reason you are here is because of me." Jenna looked at the Queen with shock and she was about to interrupt. Maia held her off, "Not me directly, it was my prophecy, which brought you to Lendaw. Specifically the prophecy: 'One will come who will be of, but not from Lendaw. One who will have the power that Anko cannot defeat. With the finding of the one, Anko's domain will cease to be forever.' You see, I am a seer. I saw this vision after your father left for Terra. On learning of your parents' death, Alistair came to believe that you were the one my prophecy predicted. You are here for your protection. It is no longer safe for you on your world. I do not know all that the future will bring. Nobody does, whatever is required of you; you will not have to do it alone," Maia paused. "We should freshen up in time for dinner. They will be expecting us."

Sometime later Jenna, the Queen and her entourage entered the dining hall, walked to their appointed seats and sat down. Jenna had sat beside Maia with Neofin on the opposite side while Alistair, Donyld and Cáel sat at the next table with a few of the elves. The third table contained the remaining elves and the dwarves. The mood in the room was jovial. The food lain upon the tables varied. There were a variety of meats and vegetables suitable for anyone's palate or desire. The drinks flowed freely and often with a choice of ale, wine, juice, or water. By late in the evening, everyone had, had their full. Jenna pushed her plate away and gave a great yawn to which the Queen responded, "To bed, young lady. I will come with you. I have taken the liberty to have your personal belongings moved to my chambers. Tomorrow is another day and we shall need our strength." All who were tired rose from their seats and left the dining hall while a handful of barflies remained behind.

CHAPTER 3

Serpent in our Mist

Come morning, Jenna rose to find the Queen already busy. "Good morning, my dear. Did you sleep well?" Jenna rubbed the sleep from her eyes and reluctantly replied, "Yes."

"Breakfast is served in the lounge over next. Please help yourself. I have further business here."

Jenna went to the lounge and helped herself to some fruit, sat on the couch and proceeded to eat. After her breakfast, Jenna went to wash up and change into clean clothes. When she was done, Jenna returned to the Queen, "Ah, I see you are ready. That is good. We need to get down to the Council chambers as soon as possible." Jenna responded with a nod, turned and left the room. The party walked down numerous corridors turning first left, then right, then right, then left and finally left again.

"Before we enter, I must warn you. Much has happened since you went to bed. Whatever occurs in the chamber it is important that you do not react. I will be with you throughout and you have support of most in the room," stated Maia as they entered the room. What Jenna saw almost floored her! The humanoid creature was hideous. It stood about nine feet high, was quite brawny and had a tail that hung to the floor. It had a face of a lizard, which was surprisingly smooth. The skin was ecru in color and scaly in nature, and his pointy teeth showed when he hissed. Nevertheless, she did what the Queen requested. Maia spoke to all in the room, "Again let us dispense with pleasantries and formalities, and let us get straight to business."

The reptilian being rose and addressed the gathering, "My Ladies and Gentlemen. I am Lisstic of the Slavidian. We are greatly offended not be invited. Perhaps this was an oversight. While it is true my people are reclusive, we care for the future of Lendaw the same you do. We concede that our history with the other races is not good. My having admitting that, I wish to offer you our assistance for a price."

The crowd in the room murmured there disbelief and distrust with each other. To say the Slavidian's relationship with the other races was not good was a complete understatement. At the least, they were a monstrous people who during the Ugland War slaughtered thousands indiscriminately.

"We have heard a rumor that one of the Weir descents has returned. It is a known fact that the Weir lineage was responsible for the murder of our Queen Symilla. She must be tried for her crime."

There was a hush in the chamber. Everyone held his, or her, breathe and waited for a response. The Queen rose and she spoke directly to the Slavidian, "Your demands have no power here. History shows that the Slavidian hold the greater guilt in these matters. War is not a pretty sight and there is guilt on both sides. We have provided the courtesy of granting you an audience. You have stated what you came here to voice. We shall not be handing anyone over regardless of whatever ill perceived wrongs that may have occurred.

"This is an outrage," raged Lisstic. "We demand justice for the murder of our Queen."

"You demand and deserve nothing. We have heard your supplications and you have your reply. You may leave now. Guards escort our guest to the gates."

If Lisstic had a weapon he would have struck her where she stood. Lisstic huffed.

How dare she dismiss me so easily? I must keep my cool for I am outnumbered here. She will pay and, so too will the girl.

Grudgingly, Lisstic ceded, "I will leave quietly this time. You should understand that we Slavidian find this intolerable. We will have our revenge." The Slavidian stormed from the room. The guards quickly followed him.

Once Lisstic was gone, the room gave a preverbal sigh.

"There can be no further doubt. The presence of the Slavidian only further confirms our theory that Anko is on the rise. We must send a party to Mount Kalla to determine the true nature of this threat. It will be a dangerous trip; people have gone missing, so I cannot appoint people for the quest. Are there any volunteers?"

Jenna stood watching and slowly raised her hand. Everyone looked at her. "I will. I volunteer since this involves my family or at the very least the Weir lineage."

Maia stared at Jenna and replied, "I cannot see how you could benefit this quest."

Jenna could see the Queen's nervousness, possibly a fear for Jenna's safety. She pondered a little while longer before she answered, "I will go anyway."

"You are so much like your father," smiled Maia, "As you wish, any other volunteers?"

One by one, the volunteers stepped forward, Alistair, Donyld, Cryall, Danyll, Durkin and Bilpin.

"Donyld, I am sorry. You cannot go. We require your assistance. We will need another volunteer."

At once Cáel stepped forward. Donyld was about to protest.

Cáel interjected him saying, "I am of age father, and I wish to go in your stead. Show me anyone here who knows how to survive better in the wild than I. This is what I have been training for most of my life."

Donyld was never more proud of his son than at this present time. He replied, "Of course you are right, you have my permission."

"We are complete with seven being a lucky number," announced Maia.

Alistair took the lead. The party would get ready for the trip and be ready to leave in seven pace-stays.

For the next few days, the castle was a buzz of activity.

Jenna found herself busier than most. Cáel had her training every day. She was up early and went to bed late. She found time just flew by.

Early on the day of their departure, Maia summoned the exploration to the atrium expressed, "We wish to give you our thanks for the loyalty and dedication in this cause. May the Fates bless you and keep you. Let us hope you return safely to us."

She then went to each in their turn handed them a personal gift and bid farewell. The Queen halted in front of Jenna and whispered, "Jenna of the Weir for a long time we have waited for your return. The stone you carry has a twin called the Tveir Stone. I offer it now as my gift to you. Use it well."

She reached over to her servant and she grasped the Iluminar handed it to Jenna who noticed that her amulet now contained two stones the Einn and the Tveir stones. I hope you do not mind, I borrowed your amulet to unite the two as to form the Iluminar. We separated them in order to prevent their accidental misplacement or misuse. They are yours, you are the rightful heir, use them well."

Jenna took the Iluminar, placed it around her neck and tucked the amulet underneath her blouse.

The Queen kissed Jenna on her forehead and bid her farewell.

The party went to the front gates where they gathered the rest of their belongings. Those who were not on foot mounted their horses, and they departed the city heading southeast.

CHAPTER 4

Craft

The companions departed the hillsides of Pandora and headed east toward the Doren River the quickest passage to Ugland and the Eastern Peninsula. By midday, the hot, Devon Sun, the larger of Lendaw's two Suns, begun to affect Jenna. Jenna began to perspire and to thirst. Jenna retrieved the flask of water from her pocket and she sipped a bit.

"Is it always this hot," enquired Jenna?

"Aye, this time of year it is," responded Cryall.

I had better conserve my water.

As the day wore on, the ground levelled off and the horses picked up the pace. The day grew hotter and hotter, and yet, the dwarves seemed remarkably unaffected by the heat and they ran alongside of the horses without trailing behind. Ever few arcs, the company paused briefly to snack and to rest. Jenna found these rest periods to be too short. She was not used to riding a horse and it showed. Her calf muscles ached. She moaned a protest each time they resumed their march. They hiked well into the evening before they concluded their trek for the day.

The next day proved just as torturous and uneventful as the previous day. They got up, ate, marched, stopped, ate, slept and repeated. Jenna did not understand how her companions could endure such an endeavor.

As the horse trotted along, Jenna reflected back on all that had occurred, "How did she find herself involved in all of this? Who was she really? Could there be some mistake.

No, Jenna could not deny what she saw and experienced these last few days. As improbable as the events of the last few days seemed, she could not deny them. She would just have to improvise and see where things led. Whatever the reason, she was drawn in this conflict. Regardless of her doubts, and she had many, she was in it for the long haul.

Alistair sensed something was wrong, "Something bothering you, my dear?"

"Nothing, everything, I don't know what to believe any more."

"Your doubt is only natural. The world as you knew it is no more. One moment you were a student and the next you are a wizard's apprentice. Now, you know there is at least another world and one where magic exists. These realities are a lot to take in. You must give yourself time to digest all that has happened. For what it is worth, you are holding up well."

"I don't know about that. I feel as if I am just going through the motions."

The two sat in silence. The company had made great progress thus far. By nightfall, they would reach Templar a tiny city at the confluence of the Donal and Clayen Rivers. It was here that they would camp for the night.

The routine continued for a little over a week when Cryall dismounted her mere, walked along side Jenna and asked, "May I speak with you a bit?"

Jenna nodded in consent.

Cryall continued, "What do you know of Magic?"

"Nothing, in my world there is no such thing as magic," responded Jenna.

"I have been asked, by Maia, to explain the history and nature of what we call 'Magic.' I would have thought Alistair would have broached this topic with you, I understand that he has not. I am not a sage on the topic, so please feel free to interrupt if you have questions." Cryall took a moment to gather her thought before she resumed, "Everything begins with the faeries. The faeries are ethereal people who are the embodiment of magic. Before the world began, they existed. The faeries divide into two divisions; namely, the faeries of light and darkness. The two forces clashed without a winner. The faeries formed an uneasy truce. Their effort did not last long. After the creation of the world and the demigods, the faeries unleashed their strife upon the demigods. They manipulated the demigods like men on the Kinknox board. The faeries procreated with the demigods and created the races, as they exist today. We elves are the eldest of such progeny followed by the dwarves, giants, ogres, and men. From these former, begot the elementals; namely, the nymphs, gnomes, sylphs and salamanders. Each race either exhibits, or summons their use of Magic by the Word. Magic is the Word, the Word is Magic and by speaking, or thinking the Word, one invokes the Magic."

"So, that was how I invoked the magic on Earth," stated Jenna, "I still don't understand exactly how could I have done it there."

"I would haphazard guess. It seems to me that you did so by the power within the Stone of Einn and the utterance of the Word. As I said, 'I am not as versed in these matters. We, elves, have magic because it is within our nature. Over time, we have learnt to increase its power by infusing the magic into natural elements within the world of Lendaw. All magical beings have the capability to embed inanimate objects such as rocks, crystals, swords, shields and the like. We, Altmer, have learnt to infuse crystals, while the dwarves have learnt to infuse metals and stones, and the Silvan learnt to infuse wooden objects and plants."

She paused and then continued, "A word of warning on the use of Magic. You may only use Magic against another Druic, or magic beings. One must never use it against Noms, or non-magical beings. This rule is a very important. By using magic against Noms, one has bad Ka, which can lead one down the dark path. One day, you will be trained in the Arts, until then keep this rule in mind."

The tiny troop travelled a long time before stopping for the day. At the camp light, they sat around and chatted while they ate. After a while, the conversation veered to questions about Terra. She explained that on Earth, there was science and that magic did not exist. She continued that once many centuries ago men believed in legends involving other races like elves, dwarves, giants, ogres, etc., regardless other than animal and plant life, only human beings inhabited the planet. Alistair interjected and he offered his impression of Earth stating he found it somewhat overwhelming – what with the busy cities, its people and vehicles going hitherto and fro, and the tall buildings, and he stated simply that he was glad to be home. Soon, it was time for the party to call it a night and to get some sleep. Durkin took first watch while the others slept. The night went by without incident.

Before they departed the camp, Alistair laid out the planned route. He warned the group to be extra vigilant as the Alyran Plains provided little camouflage. Durkin and Danyll agreed to take the lead, while Cryall and Bilpin would guard their rear. The small troop marched south.

A few hours later, Cáel went to investigate a noise he heard. After some time, he returned and he stated that he found nothing out of the ordinary. The company went forward albeit more cautiously. The next to hear the sound was Bilpin and again and another search begun without results. The cat and mouse game continued for some time until it became obvious to everyone that someone or something was playing games. The group decided it was a waste of time to keep investigating mysterious noises. They opted to continue onward and act only if there was a viable threat. By the evening, everyone was in need of rest.

The company camped at a rocked face hillside. After a quick meal, each lay down to rest and get some sleep, taking turns to keep watch.

"Get up! Wake up! They are coming."

Danyll leapt upward with bow in hand. He was not fast enough. An arrow struck him through the chest and he dropped dead with a thud. The others rose instantly and seized their weapons. They fought their opponents for several moments. Cryall was ferocious. She butchered any, and all, who approached her path. The others, likewise, fought with renewed vengeance. They cut down the enemy like reeds in the wind.

With the battle completed, they turned their attention to the gnome with weapons raised.

"Don't shoot! I am unarmed." The gnome stood two Deca in height, or just under two feet, and blended into the stone that surrounded it.

"I am Gnoz. I have been following you since you neared the Goren River. Ghob, and a few Slavidian, have been tracking you for days. I did my best to distract them and to act as a decoy. You foiled my attempts. You made too much noise. I could no longer divert your pursuers. I tried to warn you and to prevent your capture. I see I was too late."

Gnoz looked down at Danyll and the others did likewise.

Cryall knelt by her deceased brother. She took him in her arms started crying, and she began to sing:

> "Nai a nu, nai a nu, ta'am me o Delhailla.
> Don a cria.
> Nai a nu, nai a nu, sie a don'ea.
> Nai a nu, Nai a nu Danyll, Nai a nu."

After her song, Cryall wipe the tear from her eyes, arose, and she stated simply, "It is done. We must dispose of the body and move on before there are any more soldiers." They buried the body as quickly as possible, packed their belongings, picked up their weapons, and they departed.

CHAPTER 5

The Hop and Trail

The troop marched silently. They plodded through the hills and vales of the countryside. They grieved for the loss of their friend and companion. The company was miserable. The group agreed that they could all use the rest and they found a hiding place to setup camp.

Cryall sat alone, away from the camp. Jenna went to follow. Alistair gently grasped her arm, and he prevented her.

"Leave her be to mourn. It is the elven way. The song you heard is the 'Song of Sorrow.' It speaks of a great loss of one in this world, and warns of one who is to be feared in the next, and it concludes with the hope that someday they will meet again in Delhailla."

They decided to stop for the day and attempted to get some rest. Cryall and Durkin announced that they would take the first watch.

By dawn, the party ate a hasty meal, packed up and left the encampment. The small group navigated in an eastwardly direction for numerous days without any incident and they were well on their way to the Eastern Peninsula.

About a week into their journey, Jenna and her party encountered a scout of gnomes, which they easy disposed. During the scuffle, Jenna obtained a minor wound. After they tended to Jenna, the companions realized that Jenna lacked the training and the basic skills necessary for survival. From then onward, each evening, Jenna trained with one of her companions. One evening, she fenced with either Durkin or Bilpin, another evening she sparred with Cryall, and still another evening, she spent her time with Alistair who trained her in the Art of Magic.

Their journey continued until Mount Kalla appeared in the distance. Its height and span over-shadowed the countryside. Jenna had never seen anything like it. She peered around nervously to observe the others. They seemed unaffected and unconcerned. Many questions raced through her mind: What was she doing here? Why did they choose me? Was she up to the task? Was there a mistake? Her mouth was dry when she went over to Alistair.

Alistair nodded toward Mount Kalla and stated, "It is an awesome sight. If I had not grown up with it towering over me, I would have found its height to be intimidating. There is no worry."

He took her hand and smiled. He assured her that their mission was strictly reconnaissance. They needed only to observe and to listen, to retreat, and to report their findings to the Council.

After a night's rest, they renewed their journey. The danger was more apparent. Cryall and Durkin espied enemy scouts and the Order Guards movement on their excursions ahead. The company moved ever slowly and cautiously over the landscape.

By the second pace-stay, they had encountered towns and villages. They opted to stay on the outskirts in order to avoid detection.

A trip into town to replenish their stock of provisions became necessary. Jenna, Alistair and Gnoz went to trade. The others stayed behind and took shelter within the bushes. If anything were to go wrong, the others were to summon help from the Council with the Gaper, and then they were to await further orders.

The town they chose was Nepkin. It was small trading post, so they reasoned that they could blend in and remain unnoticed. Their first excursion proved uneventful. They acquired their camping supplies without incident. Alistair discretely enquired about the latest news about. The owner was polite, but was terse with them and the gathered little information. They turned their attention to food rations. They were about to enter a second shop, which was managed by a half-bred Slavidian who was half the size of a typical Slavidian. They decided to avoid that particular shop. The third shop, run by a Gnome, was proving to be tricky. The owner questioned them endless. They managed to evade his many questions. Unbeknown to them, they still managed to draw the attention of a deputy during the exchange.

While waiting for their supplies, they decided to chance one of the local inns for something to eat and to hear of the local news. The inn was 'The Hop and Trail' run by a father and daughter. The place was crowded and noisy, so they chose seating in a discrete section of the tavern, near the hustle and bustle of the kitchen doorway. They hoped that by seating here they could easily listen in on the local conversation and yet safely speak to one another without overheard on themselves. They ordered a meal and ate in silence; speaking only if spoken too. Sitting at the table, the three learnt that forces were indeed moving across the Ugland. They heard that the soldiers of the Imperial Council captured and imprisoned the some Alyrans for spying. Alistair had heard enough, he reached into his tunic for change and paid the tab. "Let's go." They quickly and quietly left the establishment.

"What was that about," Jenna asked?

"We are being watched. Gnoz put me on to it. We must get our things and move on."

After a while, they arrived at the first store invoiced the agreed supplies, paid, gathered their gear and food rations, and departed. They did the same at the other store. So far, they were in luck and no one tried to stop them.

As they neared the agreed rendezvous point, the deputy and some Imperial soldiers interrupted them. "What have we here? Look men, a Gnome with two humans, what business brings you here?"

Alistair responded, "Our business is our own. We are free citizens and have no quarrel with anyone."

"That has yet to be determined."

"We are heading to Ugland Minor. The girl's mother is ill and in need of medicine and treatment."

"A likely story, I am sure. What proof do you have that you speak the truth? There are many spies about how do we know you are not a spy for the Alyran Council?"

"I give you my word and the word of the girl. We carry no Alyran Quad; only Centri, Ugland currency, and a bit of gold."

"A bit of gold, aye, how much do you have? My men and I are in need of supplement, our wages are not what they once were. Take them!

"Arrggghh, leave me alone," squeaked Gnoz as the soldiers manhandled him and pushed him out into the street.

Jenna reached for her short sword. She was too slow and the guards were upon her before she could determine what happened.

"You are a pretty, young filly. My men and I have not had much for quite some time. You would make a fine prize."

"Take your filthy hands off me, you son of a…"

Before she could help herself, a bright flash and large explosion occurred, and she knocked the men unconscious.

"Oh my God, oh my God, what have I done, what have I done? This can't be happening. I did not mean to. What, how?"

"Jenna calm down. They still live," stated Alistair.

Durkin, Cáel, and the others came charging out of the woods.

"What the blast was that? Do you want all of Anko's forces to hear us," asked Durkin?

"It is okay Durkin. Jenna does not know her own strength. We must dispose of these soldiers before they wake up, or before someone discovers that they are missing," responded Alistair.

Gnoz stepped forward, "Leave that to me – I will need a hand."

The group gathered the unconscious men and dragged, or carried them to a bog not far from their current location.

"Jenna, I know what you are thinking. This is not your fault. While it is true this situation changes things, these men would need disposing of in any event. They would not have let us go of our own accord that much was clear by their intentions. You must control your emotions and you must learn to play out each scenario to its logical conclusion, and to act only when it is more appropriate. I would never have allowed harm to come to you. I was just waiting for a more opportune time to make my move. I was hoping for more subtle solution. You will learn these things in time, so do not you be too hard on yourself."

Alistair continued, "I think we have seen and heard enough. We had better gather the rest of our things and depart as quickly as we can. We need to get back to Alyra and inform the Council that Anko's forces are indeed gathering, that they planned the raids on the dwarves, they seized the missing men, and they likely killed them."

CHAPTER 6

Of Age

The group travelled two pace-stays. All the while, the companions chatted quietly among themselves except for Jenna who lagged behind the others.

On the third day, Cáel walked along side of her. He was not sure what to say so he opted to keep her company. He reasoned that if Jenna wanted to talk, then she would get her chance while they were walking together. They both remained silent.

By the following evening, Cáel could take no more. "Jenna, it is not your fault. The soldiers would have captured you or worst had their way with you and later killed you."

Jenna sighed, "You're right of course. I know it here," stated Jenna as she tapped her noggin, "but not here," as she stroked her heart. "It is not what I did that has me so upset, it is how I did it. I mean, I never even meant to do anything. When he grabbed my breast and said what he said, I lost it. I can't afford to lose it again. What if I hurt someone or worst kill them?"

"Alistair says you can be trained to control the magic. He would have started, if you were up to it, considering how you have been these last few days, he did not want to approach you about it. Are you going to be okay?"

She kissed and hugged him. "I will be."

They walked in silence until the most of the day, until they settled down to camp for the night. Cáel considered him-self to be the luckiest man in the world. After dinner, Jenna took first watch and the nighttime was uneventful.

By the next morning, Jenna was more her old self. She joked with Durkin and Bilpin, chatted with Cryall or discussed her lessons with Alistair.

In the three quinti of their travel back to Alyra, Jenna found her days full. They travelled during the day and trained in the evenings. The training consisted of one of either sparring with the short sword, magic lessons with Alistair or the training with Cryall in the Art of Teleclero, which included mental exercises, used to control the summoning of magic. Jenna found Teleclero the most challenging and tiring. Jenna was pleased at how far she had come in such short time, namely, her skill at the blade, her use of magic and its control. She was not alone in that assessment or at least that was what the others assured her.

As the company neared the city, a troop from the Imperial Guard came out to meet them. The captain dismounted and he approached Alistair in greeting where they soon parted from the others and the two spoke separately in whispers. The captain, later, hopped on his horse and he departed leaving the second in command to escort the exploration party back to the castle.

When Jenna entered the castle courtyard, she could sense that something was different. There was not a lot of loitering about and people seemed to have a sense of duty and urgency about them. Everyone busied himself or herself, with some chore, or duty. Jenna noted the increased guard presence. One guard had the audacity of confronting Gnoz. Alistair quickly reprimanded the guard. Now that she was back at the castle, Jenna found herself suddenly tired and hungry and not necessarily in that order. She could use something to eat and a good night's rest. As if reading her mind, Alistair informed her that her dinner would be ready in an arc's time and that afterwards they should all get some rest.

A few hours later, Jenna found herself back in her assigned room. She drew a nice warm bath and soaked for an hour this helped eased her sore muscles. She looked into the mirror, and then Jenna realized that her musculature was well defined. *All the walking, fencing and sparring she had done these last few weeks were doing her body well.* She smiled. She yawned and stretched her arms. *She was tired.* She dried herself off, changed into nightclothes, climbed into bed and passed out with exhaustion.

"Good morning Miss, my name is Taana. I will be your servant." Jenna opened her eyes to see a young girl.

"You'll be my servant, huh. Well, I don't think so. I know this is how things are in your world. In my world, all people are equal or should be in theory. When no one else is around, you may call me Jenna and treat me as a friend, or family member. All this formality makes me uncomfortable. I am not used to it."

"Yes ma'am, I mean Jenna," said Taana smiling.

"What time is it?"

"It is mid-morning."

"What! Why didn't someone call me sooner? I bet they are already meeting and no one bothered to call me," Jenna hopped from the bed. "Are these for me?" Pointing to the pile of clothes laid out on the edge of the bed.

"Yes, I am sorry; I didn't realize that you wanted to rise earlier."

"I am not mad at you Taana. Alistair will hear from me. He's over protective and he is acting as an over protective father figure."

Jenna quickly got dressed, combed her hair and left the room with Taana leading the way.

Jenna entered the Council chambers in a huff. When she realized that council had already begun, she crept up and stood beside Cryall, and in a whisper asked, "What have I missed?"

"Not much, Alistair just went over the findings of our little expedition. There is much sorrow over the loss of my brother. I do not understand why there is such an outpouring as nothing good could come of lingering over his death. Perhaps, I am much of a pragmatist."

The Council deliberated for most of the day. They debated numerous scenarios and outcomes without reaching a consensus as to what their first move should be. By nightfall, the Council agreed to remain on alert and wait for the Uglandan forces to make their first move. It was frustrating for everyone involved.

At dinner, Jenna overheard a discussion by Trevik Skay, a Council guard, to his wife that the elves and men were not ready to just sit idly by and wait for the enemy to make the first move and already the castle and the elves prepared for battle. He criticized the dwarves for not wanting to take matters to the next level and he remarked that the dwarves always tended to isolate themselves from the affairs and events of the other races of Lendaw. Jenna thought that he should have kept that information to himself. She wondered whether she should let one of the others know that Trevik was speaking inappropriately.

Jenna did not get a chance to discuss the matter further. Over the next five days, she found her time filled with practicing with the sword, sparring or training in the magic arts. It was grueling schedule still, Jenna enjoyed herself because as she alternated between Deskin for sparring, Gentwer for fencing and Dwendelmir for magic lessons; she discovered that each person had a different style of fighting, and she learnt much from each.

On the sixth pace-stay word reached Alyra, the Shadeen and the Slavidian destroyed the Dwarven stronghold of Gunnik. The news was particularly hard for Durkin and Bilpin for obvious reasons. The two brothers wished to depart the city immediately to go and determine what became of their people. The others were unable to dissuade them from their desire to leave. Thus, the two brothers left early the next morning and set out to prepare for the journey home. In the meantime, there was an emergency meeting because there was no longer any doubt that the Ugland declared war on Lendaw.

Jenna found herself with lots of free time on her hands. The planning of war and battle strategy left her excluded, as she was unable to provide anything meaningful to the discussion. She spent much of her time with Taana, which they filled playing Kinknox, reading, or going for walks about the gardens within the castle.

Jenna saw very little of her friends, and after more than two weeks, Jenna could not take her exclusion from the discussions any longer. She was determined to track down Alistair and find out what, if anything was happening. After an intensive search, she located Alistair alone in the kitchen snacking on some fruits and vegetables.

"Good day, Alistair. How are you?"

"I am well. I just dropped in to get a quick bite. I missed breakfast and lunch, and dinner is still awhile off."

"So what's happening? I haven't heard anything."

"Let's walk." Taking Jenna's arm, Alistair led her away from the kitchen and away from prying ears.

"I knew you would search for me sooner or later," Alistair chuckled, "I am just surprised it took you so long. As you may, or may not know, Anko's forces destroyed many of the Dwarven southeastern strongholds. We believe they massacred many, if not all the dwarves. There may be some survivors. Once they get a chance, Durkin and Bilpin agreed to let us know the status of the remaining dwarf forces. Our scouts in the south and the east inform us that an army is gathering with its eyes on Alyra. We have been debating as to whether we should wait here, or go and meet the threat. We have decided to do both. We will leave the sentinels to guard the castle while the army will go to meet the threat. I cannot say exactly when we will leave. I will let you know when I know when I do."

"I just feel so useless hanging around here," sighed Jenna.

"I know how you feel. Military strategy and maneuverings are not my strongest assets. I attend the meetings only because I am on the Council. We are magicians and we have a part to play in all this until then we wait. Now, I hear your lessons are going well."

"I guess, despite the fact that they are delayed for the time being."

"One more thing before I go, I have told you that there is a role in this for us. It will be dangerous to you. Only powerful magic can hope to defeat the Shadeen, there are not many who can defeat them. It is up to you and me to confront the Shadeen. Many people in court that know of this and they have sworn to provide as much protection for us as they can. We must ensure we are ready as we can possibly be. Ours is a call of service this is why we have been training you so hard. I have been lax in keeping you informed of late, and I am sorry. I promise that I will keep you in the loop from here on now."

Since having the conversation with Alistair, Jenna felt more relaxed.

Her lessons continued, with Durkin and Bilpin away, she trained more frequently with Dwendelmir. After one particular session of Teleclero, Dwendelmir pulled Jenna aside, "You are being too hard on yourself. You must learn to relax because it will come easier for you. You must make it your own a part of your subconscious. It will come in time. You have made great strides and if nobody told you recently, you are doing well. Now on to another matter, I hear that it is your birthday in two pace-stays. I have an early gift for you. For your coming of age, I have for you a Gaper. As is custom, I wanted to get you a gift you could use. It allows one to see people, or places, and it gives one the means to communicate with another over great distances." Jenna tried to protest. Dwendelmir would have none of it. "Coming of age is a once in a lifetime event, it is greatly celebrated as a milestone in one's life. You will become a Lady of Court and you will all inherit duties and responsibilities that are inherent with that position. Alistair spoke with you on this, yes?"

"Yes. Thank-you for your present, I will use it well."

"I will show you how to use it another time." Jenna already had an inkling of how to operate it as she witness Alistair using it a while back. "For now, I will take my leave. Good day to you Jenna."

On the day of her birthday, Jenna awoke to see mounts of gifts. There was a new short-sword and a knife from Gentar, new leather pants and tunic from Deskin which was the style used for travelling, and there were many new gowns and dresses laid out on the settee. Jenna spied Taana who was entering the room and this time she was not alone. "Hello my Lady. I see that you are awake. You have a busy day ahead of you and we have come to help you prepare," pointing to the other two women. Alistair requested your presence after breakfast." Jenna got dressed in her new travelling clothes, grabbed a bit of fruit off the table and left the room.

Meeting up with Alistair, Jenna responded, "Good morning, you wanted to see me?"

"Ah yes, Jenna, happy birthday, did you sleep well?"

"Thank-you, yes, I did."

"Let us take a walk. I have told you that I will keep you apprised as to what is happening. Today is your birthday, and with that, you become 'Lady Weir'. You are now an official member of court, as such; there is much you will need to learn for in order for you to fulfil your responsibilities in that title. The formalities are not the only thing you need to learn. You are required to learn the duties that come with being a Lady. I have forgotten to take part of your education into consideration. You can no longer avoid it. A warning, you will not enjoy all the pomp and circumstance that comes with being a Weir. Keep your displeasure to yourself and bite your tongue. Starting today, you begin the basics of being a Lady. Ah, here we are." Alistair knocked on the door.

"Hello," said the young girl who opened the door.

"Lady Hamilton is expecting us. May we come in?"

They entered the chamber and Lady Hamilton greeted them. They chatted for a bit and then Alistair left.

"I have tried in vain to push the importance of this training to no avail. They", waving her arms randomly, "have always insisted that you have other more important matters and you were unavailable until now. I can think of nothing more important. Heaven knows I tried. Nothing is more important than learning proper etiquette in social circumstances. One cannot be a proper lady without it." Jenna spent the next few hours torturously training in the etiquette and delicacies of becoming a Lady.

Later, in her chambers, Jenna was fuming and pacing back and forth, "What a pompous ass! I never heard so much rubbish in all my life. God, I don't know how you all can stand it?" Taana kept quiet all the while trying to get Jenna ready for the ball.

To Jenna's thinking, the ball went off without a hitch, that is, if you didn't consider the fool that she made of herself while trying to dance. After the ball, Jenna heard one titbit of important information. Lord Donyld would be heading north to try to recruit the Silvan, the Wood elves, to join the cause to and stand in the fight against Anko.

At breakfast the next morning, Jenna learnt that Donyld expected Cáel to join him on his quest to secure more re-enforcements, which implied that Cáel would be leaving in about two days. Jenna was somewhat shocked at this because she believed that Cáel would join them when they went to battle. She had no to reason to make that assumption. She just did.

Puzzled at this, Jenna reflected on how she felt for him. Jenna conceded that she liked him. After all, what wasn't to like? Cáel was tall and handsome. He was funny and he had a great smile. He was a good friend and a confident and nothing more. She was too young and she was not ready to settle down. Finally, she convinced herself that if Cáel went with his father, then she would miss him and that was all, at least that was what she told herself. Deep down inside of herself, she knew it bothered her more than she wished to admit. Deep down, she decided that if things were to get more serious, then that would not be a bad thing.

A quintus, about a week, after Donyld left north, word reached Alyra of another attack in the small city of Ligwick and there were few survivors. That evening, Alyra declared war on Ugland and its allies. As sad as it was to hear the news, Jenna did learn that Cáel remained behind at his father's insistence and selfishly she was glad.

Since they had already been preparing for battle, it would only take another week for the army to get ready to depart the castle for Kinell to meet with the elves.

In the meantime, Jenna's time consisted of training and more training, which unfortunately for Jenna, included the dreadful lessons with Lady Hamilton. She cherished her fighting lessons the most as they now consisting of fighting with protective gear. This new aspect provided her with greater challenges that she found she rather enjoyed.

CHAPTER 7

The Dream

After a long and arduous march, the Alyran army led by Lord Hamilton halted for the night. The company was in need of rest. They pushed themselves to the point of fatigue. The elves expected them in Kinell in four quinti. With the supplies and equipment, the schedule was very tight. Lord Hamilton had no choice other than to push his men to the point of exhaustion. It was approximately two quinti into their journey south while most of the camp was either sleeping, or nodding off to sleep that they were jolted awake.

"Jenna, Jenna, wake up," implored Taana.

"What?"

"You were having a nightmare and screaming. It was an awful, cold, chilling scream and it is still creeping me out," stated Taana. "What were you dreaming about that would cause such a fright?"

The yelling woke Cáel who was only now coming as he followed Alistair, Cryall and Gnoz into the tent.

"That is what I would like to know as well, Taana," stated Alistair as he entered the tent. "I could hear you from the middle of the camp."

"I am not too sure. It is somewhat hazy right now. It seemed so real. I could have sworn I was awake. I cannot believe it was just a dream."

"It may not have been," replied Alistair, "Take your time. Tell me in as much detail as you can, what did you see in your dream?"

"Well, I will try. As I said, previously, 'It's somewhat blurry now,' let me see. I was some place I have never been before, so I did not recognize it. Cáel, you and I were travelling through a cavern with the others trailing when all of a sudden we were surrounded by three Shadeen. Alistair and I confronted the Shadeen, then there was a great explosion, and then they were dead. At first, I was elated at defeating the Shadeen, and then I turned around to witness Cryall and Cáel falling into an abyss. Oh, Alistair, I saw them fall to their death." Jenna was sobbing, so Alistair approached her and placed his arm on her shoulder.

Jenna continued to shake and sob profusely. Cáel rushed over to Jenna, while Alistair stepped back and he let Cáel hold her. "It is only a dream, Jenna. It's only a dream," Cáel murmured.

"What if it wasn't? It could be a premonition. I cannot stand to lose you. I love you."

"I know. I love you too. It was only a dream. If it was more, then we know what will happen and we will be able to prepare for it," looking at Alistair hopefully. Alistair remained silent. When Jenna calmed down a little, everyone except Cáel departed, which left him to care for Jenna. After a while, the two fell asleep in each other's arms.

Jenna isolated herself from the others. The continuous rain for the next three quinti only dampened her mood further. She tried all she could to stay away from the others especially Cáel. She dreaded any encounters with him and she avoided any eye contact with him whenever they met. When Cáel could not take it any longer, he grabbed Jenna by her arm. She yanked free of his grip. She yelled at him to stay away. She screamed that she never loved him and never would, and insisted that he leave her alone.

Cryall advised Cáel to give Jenna some time to come to terms with the vision and to give her as much leeway as possible.

The next day, neither one got to brood over her or his differences, while the rain continued to fall and the company trudged along in a slow, agonizing pace through the thick, deep mud, Galex surfaced from the clouds. Men run! Take cover! Take cover! The men and horses hurried to get out of the way. With an agility of a man far younger than he was, Alistair leapt to the defense. With his staff raised, he shot at the rider and the Gargon hitting it squarely on the mark causing it to howl in rage and its rider to fumble. Jenna took her chance and raising the Iluminar released its energy. The power of the Iluminar burned at the shield Galex that instantly rose. The force pounded against the shield and the sky seared and tingled. The power grew exponentially, the shield collapsed and the fire engulfed everything in its wake. Galex and the Gargon were no more, and Jenna fell to her knees in utter exhaustion. Alistair rushed to her side, yelling, "Men stay alert there may be others in the vicinity." Couching down beside Jenna, Alistair invoked a protective shield around them stating, "Jenna you are safe, rest and regain your strength."

Three arcs later, they departed from the site since they could not risk staying put any longer. As they travelled, they pondered all that occurred that morning. "What I cannot understand was why Galex would show himself as he did," stated Alistair. They debated among themselves Alistair, Jenna, Cryall, and Cáel as to the nature and reason of the attack. It did not make sense. Alas, they could not reach any consensus as to why he would attack nor the reason he came alone and by evening they settled down for the night.

A quinti later, there was another commotion within the camp. "Gentar, what is the meaning of this ruckus?"

"Forgive me, Sir Hamilton, we caught Trevik Skay wandering outside the camp and when we tried to question him, he ranted that he was Council Guard and that we had no right to question him. We decided to present him to you," stated Gentar.

"Quite right, Skay what were you doing outside the grounds this morn?" asked Lord Hamilton.

"Oh, morn Sir Hamilton, hum nothing, I was, uh, doing nothing. I, hum, could not sleep that is all. I, uh, went for a walk to clear my head."

"Lord Hamilton, we found this on him and he was whispering into it," informed Gentar handing him a Gaper.

"What is it?" enquired Hamilton.

"It is a Gaper. It is more than a mirror and it will have a partner. It is a communication devise used conversing over large distances," interjected Alistair.

"Trevik what are you doing with such a device?"

"Alistair, I hum… it was uh…" Trevik paused and remained silent thereafter.

"Well Charles, it is quite obvious that he was communicating with someone. The question is, 'Who?'"

"Skay, make this easy on yourself man, and tell us who you spoke to a little while ago," implored Hamilton.

Trevik stood still and he kept silent.

"I saw him," stated Cáel as he approached the discussion.

"What is that Cáel?" asked Alistair.

"I was out for a stroll, to clear my head, when I heard Jenna's name mentioned further ahead, so I followed the voice until I discovered him speaking to an image in the mirror. From my vantage point, I could not tell to whom he was speaking. As I neared, I heard him mention Donar. When I confronted Skay, he denied it and he started to protest, and that was when Gentar and his men appeared."

"That is a lie. I did no such thing," declared Trevik.

"You did, I believe that you have betrayed us today, and that you have been doing so for quite some time. I think you are the informant that we have been searching. Donyld and I long suspected someone at court of abetting the Shadeen. Until today, we did not know whom. Now, I believe we have our answer. Why would you betray our kindred so?"

Trevik hesitated. At first, Skay attempted to deny the allegations against him, but then he thought better of it. They had caught him in the act. Finally, he relented, "I have been Council Guard for many years and each year, they denied my promotion."

"What did you tell them, Skay?"

There was an awkward silence.

"You are right of course. I have been spying for Donar. I informed him all of the Court's decisions that I attended. I have done so for many moons." He sobbed uncontrollably, "I have mentioned the girl, that it was her that slays Galex."

Trevik paused briefly before he continued, "When Donar last confronted you on Terra he witnessed the girl coming to your aide. It was then that Donar surmised that the girl posed a greater threat to himself and the other Shadeen. To test his theory he sent Galex to discover if his hunch was correct. Galex got cocky. He overstayed his welcome and he died in the process. Thanks to me, Donar knows the truth. Alas, I now regret my involvement. I wish I had done things differently. It is too late.

The past cannot be undone," Trevik pulled out a dagger. Before he could act, Cáel was upon him. The two briefly fought. The two struggled and rolled upon the ground when Cáel accidentally struck him down.

"I wish you did not have to do that. I hoped to question him and to discover if he knew how Donar was able to track my location. Since we know our betrayer, I think I have that puzzle solved as well."

Alistair reached into his tunic and pulled out an amulet of the finest quality ever seen with blue gold containing amber and garnet settings. "See these symbols etched here and here," as he pointed near the north garnet stone. I have been wondering what the possible meaning and significance these two icons as he pointed at the top of the amulet. I have never seen their like before and I have a great understanding of semiotics – the study of symbols. I do not know their exact meaning though I believe they are a means, through Magic, of tracking the carrier of this particular amulet. You see, Skay is not only a Council guard. He serves as my personal guard as well. He presented me with this gift at last winter's solstice celebrations. Ever since then, the enemy has always been one move ahead of me. Yes, it makes perfect sense. Donar has been using both the amulet and Trevik's information to track my every move."

"Why that means we are not safe," exclaimed Charles.

"No we are not. Charles, I must leave and I must go soon. Take the company south-west through Doren Gorge travel six pace-stays before you head east to Ganoll. I will go east and act as decoy. When it is safe to do so, then I will go south to Kinell and meet up with the elves. We will meet at Ganoll in ten pace-stays, ten. We will decide, at that time, what our next move will be."

"Doren Gorge is a precarious passage. What you are asking for will be next to impossible with all these men and supplies."

"Precisely and that is the reason you must take that route. The journey is treacherous. The enemy will never suspect we would take this passage."

"But…"

"No buts, Charles, this is urgent and I do not have time to debate the matter further. You must ensure that the army arrives at Ganoll at all cost. I know, I am asking the impossible. You must do it. There is no other way. Take this," as Alistair handed a crystalline shard to Hamilton, "you will need to use it at the appropriate time."

"What is this? How do I?" Alistair interjected, "No time to explain, you will know when and how to use it when the time is right." Charles pondered for a moment, "You're right of course. I will see to it."

"I will take my leave then," turning to go, Alistair exclaimed, "Jenna you must come with me."

"Not without us," insisted Cryall, Cáel, and Gnoz. "We are coming with you."

"I was hoping to make a quick get-a-way. It will be faster and easier to travel with two."

"You are not leaving without me," stated Cáel "Jenna is mine to protect."

"And I made a vow to Maia that I would protect Jenna at all cost," Cryall replied.

"I have previously promised. I will travel with you as well," replied Gnoz.

Alistair tried to protest. They abruptly cut him off.

"There is no sense in debating further. I believe I speak for the others when I say that we are all coming with you," said Cryall.

"Very well, then grab what you need and let's get going. We will need steeds. We must put as much distance between us and the army before Donar learns that we are on to him. We will be the diversion that the army needs while it makes its way southward. If Donar figures out that we know he can track us, then my plan will not work. It needs the element of surprise if we are to succeed, and it is imperative that the army arrive at Ganoll as safe as possible; our winning this battle relies on it doing so."

An arc later, the two groups departed ways with the smaller heading left while the larger headed right.

CHAPTER 8

Cocidius

As Alistair confronted Trevik about the Gaper, the two dwarf brothers neared dwarf territory.

Bilpin and Durkin travelled almost four quinti to reach the Andar Mountains. The Uglandan troops roamed the southlands. Their journey had been a perilous and a difficult one. The two continuously changed routes to avoid their detection or capture.

One evening, while resting, Bilpin and Durkin debated over what their next move should be. In true Durkin form, Durkin asserted that they should just make their way to Gunnik to find any survivors. Bilpin being more level headed explained that it would be too risky just going to Gunnik. He continued to explain that the number of troops patrolling the area made that choice a non-option. He further rationed that there were only two of them and they were hopelessly out numbered. Bilpin determined that they would need to seek some type of advantage if they were to succeed in freeing their people.

"I have a plan. It is not a great plan and I still need to iron out the kinks. I believe I may be grasping at straws; it is also our only hope. We should get some rest. Tomorrow we head to Haugr Passage."

"Bilpin, I have never heard of such a place."

After two arcs sleep, the two brothers continued on their travels.

One the second pace-stay, Durkin whined, "Brother, why this way by Odinson's hammer. It would have been easier to go by Erek's Passage.

You still haven't explained why Haugr Passage and why I have never heard of it?"

"I explained earlier. We cannot trust the known passages through the Andar Mountains. Our people have been betrayed."

"So you say, and you may be right. I just wish you'd had picked an easier route. How is it you know of this route? I have travelled far and wide in my many journeys and I have no knowledge of it."

"The legends dear brother, you never were good at history or our folklore for that matter. Krom told me a tale once of Trod's Odyssey. Do you know of it?"

"It is true schooling wasn't one of my greatest strengths, so I can't say I have."

"According to Crom there are few people who have heard the tale and the essence of it just might be the key to our salvation."

"I don't get your meaning, brother. How do mean?"

"Krom told me of Trod's hammer a weapon so powerful that it could strike down an army with one blow. I mean for us to find this weapon."

"Are you nuts? Even if it exists, which I highly doubt, it could be anywhere."

"Legend states that after the Orkan War, Trod Odinson fled with the remainder of our people through Haugr's Passage. It was there that they took refuge. Eventually, they established a settlement there. It took them nine hundred years to rebuild our culture and our cities. Then for some strange reason, our people had to flee. It is unknown why they had to leave. We only know that they departed and they did so in a hurry. In their haste to leave, Trod and the hammer were lost. Shortly thereafter, our people resettled in Gunnik deep within the Andar Mountains." He paused to give Durkin time to absorb the tale. After a little while, he continued, "I believe that the Haugr Passage is where we will find what we are seeking. The ancient symbol is similar to the one used in the new dialect. I think that the two words translate to the same meaning – the words for high passage. The answer was staring us in the face all this time – under our very noses in-fact. The Haugr Passage is the highest passage in the Ander Mountains."

"No one has used the Haugr Passage in eons."

"Exactly Durkin. That is the key part. The question you have to ask yourself is: 'Why, why isn't it used anymore?' There must be a reason. I believe that after our people fled, they avoided this area and kept it out of known history; whatever occurred here must have been too horrible the inhabitants to remember because there is no written or spoken mention of it in modern history."

"Well if that is the case, then we must be mad to be seeking this hammer."

"Mad or desperate, it doesn't matter anymore. Our people are lost. We may well be the two last dwarves on the planet. In either event, if we are to find some survivors, then we must have some advantage against our enemies if we have any hope of existence as a race. What else have we got to lose?"

"Aye, I see your point, nothing I guess. How are we to know what to find?"

"There is a myth that the hammer will seek out a champion and that it will want to be found."

The two brothers continued on their journey and they stopped due to exhaustion.

"Brother we must camp here; I cannot take another step forward."

The two quickly set up camp and then they lay down to rest.

Their journey continued for a few more pace-stays. The rough terrain made their travels difficult and slow.

On the fourth night after the tale, Durkin slept and dreamt a dream. He dreamt of a cave with a seamless door. How he got in, he could not remember and he could not find Bilpin anywhere. The cavern was enormous – a whole city could sit within its walls, and it appeared as one had. Dirt, dust and some fragmented stonework laid upon the ground. The city was ruined and it lay in shambles. *What in the name of the gods happen here?*

He travelled deeper and deeper into the inner working of the cavern. It was more of the same. He was about to turn back when he heard it - a distant faint roar, then he heard it repeatedly.

As it neared, the sound got louder and louder. Soon, the walls shook with each bellow.

What was that? Spying the creature, he quickly and quietly crept back against the wall on one side of the cavern – he hoped with all his might that it did not spot him. He so desperately wished that he could blend to its walls. The creature making its way forward was unlike anything he had ever seen or ever dreamt. It was monstrously hideous and mammoth in size. As it entered the cavern, it quickly filled the room and it was nearly upon him.

How could something like that exist? He did not have time to ponder the question further for the creature set upon him and he made his escape along the wall to the far left side in near panic.

How am I to get out of here? As if to answer, he heard a voice clear as day. "Call for the Mjolnir!"

Before he could utter a word, he felt the hilt of an axe strike his palm. The power of the axe renewed his courage and his resolve. He gripped the axe, he turned to face the creature and he stood against the gigantic monster. The creature upon eyeing the axe, initially stepped back in hesitation, and then quickly gained its resolve, took a swipe with its left claw at Durkin who swerved right to avoid its hit and turning around struck the creature on the horn in its trunk. The creature howled in agony as the monster smashed into the side of the cavern. In response, the cavern rumbled and crumbled from the impact of the beast. Undaunted, the creature stood up, shook its head and came forward again albeit with a little more caution. As the two foes circled each other, Durkin tripped and he nearly stumbled. He regained his footing before the creature could strike. Durkin pounded the creature in the side of the head, it went down with a crash, and the chamber trembled.

"Now, do it now. Now is your only chance! Strike the heart." Before he could reason it out, Durkin rushed forward and with a mighty blow struck the creature in the chest. The creature roared and groaned, and then lay unconscious on the floor.

"It is not dead if that is what you are thinking. I do not think anything will kill it."

"Who are you? Show yourself!"

A moment later, the apparition appeared before him.

"I am Trod, son of Odinson, or what remains of me anyway. I am a shadow of my former self. I am neither alive nor dead. I exist only between the worlds. My cursed is to wait for a successor. Perhaps my search is over and I can finally rest."

"What? How did I get here?

"The Mjolnir called you. It chose you."

This was Monyahr the first city after the Orkan War. I led what remained of our people to rebuild our society and our city. We worked for hundreds and hundreds of years. The city was beginning to take shape. One had never seen such brilliance and artisanship, yet the people were unsatisfied. They wanted more. In order to meet the resources required to beautify the city, we dug deeper and deeper until we unknowingly release the Cocidius. Our people fled to safety while I tried and failed to slay the demon. Over the years, I weakened and laid in slumber until my replacement came to release me – you.

"Me!" Bah, you got to be joking!"

"You hold the Mjolnir that is proof enough that you are the rightful heir because only the one of pure heart and who has no malice may yield the axe."

"I… *sigh*. How did I get here? The last thing I remember is going to sleep."

"The Mjolnir summoned you in your sleep. You travelled here. Now it is time for you to go. You must get to Lagr Gardr and gather the remainder of our people. My work is finished here and it is time for me to retire."

"Durkin," yelled Bilpin.

Durkin turned to the sound of his brother's voice, "Wait one moment Bilpin."

Upon turning back toward Trod, Durkin realized he was outside of the cave and Trod was gone.

The entire event seemed like a dream, except for the fact that Durkin held the axe in his hand.

CHAPTER 9

Loren

About the same time that Durkin and Bilpin were seeking out the Haugr Passage, Donyld reached the Northern Escarpment.

"Easy Dora," stated Donyld as he stroked the horse beneath him.

She senses it too. Someone is watching us.

"Come out; show yourself! I come in peace and glad tidings."

"Let's move forward carefully Dora. We do not know what is ahead."

They traversed gingerly through the thick forest of Trillemara for nearly half a par-stay. Donyld had never travelled these parts before, so he had no idea what to expect.

"What to expect? A lot I'd say."

"Sal Tel Doe e Paevast," greeted Donyld.

"And greetings to you. Caidor at your service," bowing mockingly, "You shall come with me, I would advise you not to try anything as my men are nearby."

The two travelled further into the woods. Donyld had a great sense of direction yet he could no longer determine his whereabouts was – first left, then right, and so on until after a while he could no longer discern to which direction they were heading.

"Don't worry, my friend, it is the enchantment protecting our lands which prevents your knowing where we are. You are safe as long as you are with me. Many would travel through these lands forever and die before they ventured near our city."

"How is it you seem to know what I am thinking? Can you read my mind?"

"It is not your mind. No, it is your mannerisms; they betray you. I can read your every intention."

"I guess I had better control my emotions and expressions then."

Caidor laughed.

"We are nearly there. You must dismount and hand me your weapon as a sign of good faith. I promise you will get it back. You are part elf, so I suspect that you do not require a weapon."

A little bit further on they reached a great ladder.

"We head up from here. Tyrall, see to his horse," who seemed to appear from nowhere, "As you wish Captain." Caidor handed the weapons to Tyrall.

Donyld and Caidor ascended the vine ladder. Upon reaching, the top Donyld could not believe his eyes. A city the likes of which he had never seen before, here within the trees. The intertwining and the weaving of the tree branches formed the structures and houses occupied by the Lórien. The forest vegetation shaped the rooftops and provided a shelter against the natural elements. It was a marvel to behold.

"Yes, it is an awesome sight. At first sight, it takes one's breathe away. Come, the Court is expecting us."

The two walked toward the great hall. Many elves espied the stranger within their mist.

"You must forgive them. We are a solitary people by nature and we are not used to strangers within our walls."

"I guess I cannot blame them for be curious."

"My Lord Caidor, Her Majesty the Queen will see you now."

"Thank-you, Ada."

The two entered the great hall and headed to the throne. Caidor bowed, "My Lady Arthel. May I introduce… I am sorry; I forgot to ask – what is your name?"

"Lord Donyld, my Lady," replied Donyld. "Sal Tel Doe e Paevast," he greeted the Queen.

"Sal Tel Doe Donyld," we have been expecting you or an emissary from Erenhil. Welcome to the Court of Loren, we know why you are here. The danger is greater than you ever imagined. From Ugland lands, to the territories of the dwarves and to Denlup, the scourge spreads like a cancer that will not stop. It will continue until it consumes all of Lendaw. Would that we work together, to defeat the darkness that threatens to overshadow the face of the world; however, suspicion and mistrust abound to keep our peoples apart. There is fault on both sides. I know. How are we overcome this rift? What could you possibly have to bridge the gap between us?"

"A gift for my Lady, here is the Eridu," as he handed the golden cone to Caidor.

Concern filled the room and the tension increased ten-fold. "Where did you come upon this? We haven't seen this object for many ages."

"It was for a better word acquired from Grendel. Actually, we retrieved from his dead hand. During his failed attempt to steal the Lunayr, the source of Alyra's defensive shield, he died.

"Then we should make our apologies. We believed that Erenhil had procured the Eridu for itself."

"I can assure you we did not. Our people were unsure of its significance until we came upon the Dictum Lexicon, the ancient scrolls of ages past. It was not until number of years later that we discern its significance. By then, our people had long quit associating with each other. Am I right in guessing it is the Seed of Life?"

"It is. Do you know of its significance?"

"A suspicion only, I believe it to be 'The seed of life?' Specifically, it is the means of regrowth should this forest fall."

"That is a good guess. Should Lórien and most of its people fall, we need only plant the Eridu and Lórien will grow anew. It is ancient magic. It is our life line."

During their conversation, Donyld heard a commotion out in the hallway. Suddenly, the doors of the great hall burst open and a creature, like a giant tree, came charging toward the Throne. Instinctively, Donyld shoved those beside him aside and he let out a surge of power temporarily halting the creature. He was ready to attack the creature further. The soldiers seized him by the arms and implored him to stop.

"You may stop now Donyld. The creature you see before you is kindred. It means no harm. It was a test. We had to discover where your true loyalties lay. We are all kindred here," explained Arthel.

Confused, Donyld released the spell.

"I am Brackenwood kin to the Loren. I am a Treent. You may think of me as a living tree."

"Like a tree nymph," mumbled Donyld.

Blackenwood grew enraged and shouted, "I am not a common tree nymph". Then he eased and continued, "I, and my kind, are guardians of Lórien."

"I beg your pardon," responded Donyld, "I meant no insult, nor no harm — the spell was a defensive move. It would not have hurt you."

"No offense taken," laughed Brackenwood, "and your spells could not hurt me here where the forest is thickest. It feeds and nurtures me. You would have to destroy most of the forest to cause any real injury to my person and I doubt one lone person could accomplish that feat."

"As you were saying the traitor Grendel was trying to steal the Lunayr. This news and the fact that he had the Eridu on his possession are most troubling, most troubling indeed. This could only mean that he was employed by Anko or one of his agents."

"Indeed my Lady. This is another reason why I have come to Lórien. Our peoples are in danger. I implore you we must unite for the common good. If we do not stand together, then we can have no hope of stopping this blight."

"Donyld, as previously mentioned we are aware of the plight affecting Lendaw. This plague will spread until all of Lendaw is infected. You come to seek our help and we gladly give it. As we once were, so shall we be again. We will reunite. We are elves, and as such, we are keepers of the land. Since the creation of the world, the creators charged us with it care and its protection. We are bound to the land and the land is bind to us. If Lendaw falls, then we elves die too. We see the scourge moving throughout the lands. It must not spread or all will be lost. We require preparation time before we set out to meet this threat. We would hear what the Erenhil would have us do. What has Maia planned?"

For the next two pace-stays, they discussed strategy and they reviewed their plans.

During one such session, Donyld summarized the events of the past few cycles. He told of the prophecy; Alistair's quest; the Weir's return to Lendaw and how Jenna may be the fulfillment of the aforementioned prophecy. This former news filled the Loren with awe. The Weir's return to Lendaw was joyous news indeed and it provided them with the comfort that this war may be winnable.

On the day of Donyld's departure from the Lios, Queen Arthel assured him that the Loren would follow him in two pace-stays. She asked that he precede them and arrange for their arrival. She saluted him and stated, "Paevast Donyld, elf brethren and friend."

Donyld bowed, "Paevast Arthel Queen of Lórien. Ryae di Lórien."

Arthel smiled at the use of the old language, "Tyrall, take your men and escort Donyld safely to the southern edge of Trillemara. From there, he can find his own way back to Alyra."

"Aye my Lady, your wish is my command."

CHAPTER 10

Mudluck

Alistair and his party, meanwhile, travelled east and along the way they decided to go to Mudluck, the habitat of the gnomes, and beseech King Griebel to reconsider and to join the alliance against Anko and his forces.

"Alistair, it is three pace-stays to Mudluck perhaps I should go ahead and prepare for your arrival. I doubt Griebel would welcome strangers to the city. We are a solitary people and we tend to avoid outsiders whenever possible, that is to say, nearly always."

"Gnoz, we will meet at Katell Loge."

"Okay Alistair, if I am not there, then you will know something is wrong, so don't wait for me. I am not expecting trouble. In times like these, one can never know."

"We should rest and let Gnoz time to reach his people," stated Alistair to the others.

Jenna asked, "Alistair, what if they do not want to meet with us? What then?"

"We move south Jenna. We still need to get to Kinell and then from there to Ganoll to meet with our forces there."

The little group supped and napped for half a pace-stay before moving on. They travelled the rest of the journey without any incidents.

At Katell Loge, the party took shelter and waited for Gnoz. When he did not appear that next few pace-stays, they knew that there was trouble,

Alistair informed the others stating, "It appears that Gnoz's fears were just. There must be an issue at Mudluck. I think we should scout it out."

The party departed the safety of Katell Loge and crept their way to Mudluck keeping an eye out for any sign of danger. The danger was already there.

As they approached Mudluck, the Order Guard commanded them to stop.

Alistair scrutinized the surrounding troop before he told his companions to stand down. They obediently complied with Alistair's request, and stood down, as did the soldiers.

"Who do I have the honor of addressing?"

"I am Captain Novak, Captain and Chief of the Order Guard."

"I am Marpole and these are my companions. We are Kali: 'The Free folk'. As you know, we are a nomadic people. The Kali have no allegiance to any one nation or people. We travel from city to city for commerce and trade. We care not for the concern of others. We only wish to trade."

Novak assessed the group of humans and elves.

"What brings thee to these parts?"

"I may ask the same. What is the Order Guard, the O.G., doing in Mudluck? The Mudluckan are a peaceful folk."

"Our business is our own. The O.G. answer to no one, now answer my question."

"We are going to the Port of Jaffa and then onward to the Isle of Mytha to get away from what we all know is coming. We do not want any part of the coming war. Our departure is delayed because my companion Napili, who is new to this area, has accidently ate the root of the Circuta and she requires medicine before we can continue onward."

Danyll discretely nudged Jenna. When prodded, Jenna let out a moan, she grabbed her stomach and she bent over.

"Follow us and do not veer off. We will take you to get the medicine you require, and then you must be off. Visitors are no longer welcomed here."

The little group followed the Captain into the lair of city. Alistair and the others observed the Mudluckan as the entered.

The gnomes worked the pits and mines. The guards threatened and beat those that rest. They looked haggard. They appeared emaciated. They were skeletal and lanky. They had sunken eyes. The clothes they wore were mere rags. The gnomes appeared downtrodden. They looked defeated.

"Clearly, the Mudluckan have been a captive people for quite a while," though Alistair who glimpsed the others and noticed that they were thinking along similar lines.

The party descended into the earth still further. The caverns veered off in every direction nonetheless the group continued down the hall of the cave until at last the came to a key hole.

"Loopwyn, your services are required."

"Bah, what is it? Can you not see that I am busy?" As she stepped out the key hole, "Ah, strangers, what can I do for thee?"

"Are you Curer here? My companion is in need of medicine. She mistakenly ate of the Circuta root."

"Come in, dearie; let me look at you then. It may be a bit of a squeeze for you and you will have to bend down a bit. It is tight. You are lean, so you should fit. The rest of you will have to stay put. We'll be done in a bit."

Jenna followed Loopwyn through the key hole and into a labyrinth. Jenna was awed when she saw the network of mazes.

"The O.G. hasn't a clue. We could sneak out this way and be gone long before it dawned on them."

"Then why don't you? You and your people could flee to freedom."

"Where could we go? We have no other home. Besides, King Griebel has forbidden it," sigh, "You look quite well for someone who has eaten the Circuta root. What are you and your companions up to?"

"We are looking for a friend who came here about a pace-stay ago perhaps you can answer my query, have you seen Gnoz?"

"Aye, lass that I do, he is no longer here. He was. The OG sent him to the Pits of Muwtag. I treated him before they sent him away. They had me treat him in his cell. I think they suspected there were caverns, which would provide a means of escape or maybe it was just easier to treat him there. In either event, he is gone."

"We were to meet Gnoz at Katell Loge. He never showed. We came to determine the reason for his absence."

"So you are the friends he hoped would not arrive, you should not have taken the risk. He did indicate you might show up. You must leave as soon as possible. It is not safe for you here. My people are weak and fearful, and there are spies among us who would blab on anyone who tried to mount a resistance to the OG. Poor Gnoz tried just that."

"Before I go, I must know. What has happened to Mudluck?"

"Simple, the OG came. They want our minerals, ores, and our alchemists for weapons for the coming war. We never put up a resistance and now look at our lot. We are slaves."

Loopwyn pointed, "We must return you to your friends. If we stay any longer, then they will suspect that we are up to something."

Jenna and Loopwyn passed through the key hole and into the outer chamber.

Once Jenna settled on her horse, the Order Guards escorted the little group to the outskirts of Mudluck with a warning never to return.

Alistair and his group headed west for one pace-stay before turning south toward Kinell to meet with the elves. Along the way, Jenna discussed her conversation with Loopwyn.

CHAPTER 11

Meglog

Meanwhile at the Doren Gorge, the Alyran army marched southward through its varying crevices keeping alert to the slightest ambiguity. The troops travelled thusly for more than three pace-stays and were growing apprehensive.

The men feel it too. There is something evil lurking in these parts. Why Alistair insists we go this way is beyond me. He knows, as well as I, folklore speaks of Meglog the beast that dwells in these blackened walls a creature of another time and another world, and a survivor of a war too horrible to imagine where nothing could survive, nothing that is, except Meglog itself. Only two pace-stays and we will depart this dreadful place.

He sighed. Instinctively he reached into his pocket.

Good, it is still there. The shard felt like a dagger.

He realized that he felt great comfort in the knowledge of possessing any type weapon.

The anticipated trouble that most men expected did not materialize. The night passed without incident, and in the morn, the troop marched onward for the remainder of the day. With the coming dusk, an eerie fog filled the canyon.

The horses were first to sense it. They pulled back, snorted and neighed with anxiety long before the appearance of the creature. It seemed to appear from out of nowhere. It struck down the first line of men with two quick blows of its mighty fist. The rest of the army scattered in every direction trying to seek some shelter from the beast.

The beast was hideous. It stood six stories, had blackened skin of leather that looked scarred beyond anything recognizable, it had talons for hands and feet, and long, thick, jointed arms and legs; it hunched down such that its head centered it torso and it had three eyes, two horns and long blotchy hair.

"A demon," whispered Hamilton.

Charles jumped from his horse with sword in hand.

Before he could act, a few elves within the ranks casted their spells in the hopes of ensnaring or maiming the creature to enable their escape. They failed. No matter what incantations or enchantments they attempted, none worked. If anything, their incantations only infuriated the creature more.

It roared. "Fools, your spells do not affect me. I existed long before Magic and I will remain ever after. I am Meglog: The Goetia. I survived the fires of Armageddon. I am the first and the last."

Meglog swung its right arm to the men approaching from that flank. It struck and killed those within reach and the rest quickly retreated, "fall back, fall back!" yelled Charles.

Charles turned to face the creature. He was one man against a demon.

"Ah, the brave one, come forward little one if you dare, come and step forward."

Every instinct instructed Charles to flee with his men save that of their safety. Only the desire of the safety of his men permitted him to move forward. He prodded with heavy foot until every muscle in his legs and lower back ached with fatigue. When he was just out of reach of the demon, he stopped.

The two foes stood face to face. Each assessed the attributes and strength of the other.

"Who braves to confront the powerful Meglog?"

"I am Lord Hamilton of Alyra. I respectfully ask for passage for my men and me. There is war south, we need quick passage and mean you no harm. All of Lendaw is threaten by the scourge that ravishes our world. We go to meet this threat and to prevent its infection."

"What care I for war? There will always be war or rumors of war. It is of no concern for me. Even if this world passes, I will continue."

"There is one who, when he conquers all of Lendaw, may pose a danger to you in the future. His name is Anko and he will not rest until all kneel before him. If he discovers you here, then he may want your submission."

"My submission, ha, do not make me laugh. No one can hurt me, nor break me. I bow to no one."

While they conversed, they two circled each other contemplating on their next move.

"The beast is too confident. It believes itself to be invincible and he just might be," thought Charles, "Hold it. What's that?"

He spotted something on the nape of the creature as it turned its head to observe on the troops at its left. Then an idea occurred and Charles knew what he had to do.

The question was, "How to act?" That was the tricky part.

He sensed that the creature tired of this little contest.

Charles espied Vidal to his left and slightly nodded. Vidal discretely took out a bow, loaded an arrow and quickly aiming for the right eye, he fired.

As Meglog clasped his eye and howled in agony, Charles made his move.

He dropped his sword, reached into his pocket, grasped the shard in his hand, and scaled the right half of the creature using the locks of its mane to pull himself up until he sat upon the back of the creature.

"The indignity, the outrage," bellowed Meglog with rage.

Before the demon could act, Charles thrust the shard into its fleshy nape.

The monster yelled and began to buck until it managed to throw Charles forward and off its back.

Charles hit the ground with a deadly thud and was no more. He looked down upon his body, which lay crushed beneath his feet. The rescue attempt had cost him dearly. He now lived as a phantom. Woefully, he realized that he and Meglog now existed in unison — One could not live without the other and neither of them could die. Charles soon realized that he could temporary control the creature's thoughts and movements and he used this knowledge to help free his troop.

Charles' murmured voiced breezed through the air. It urged the men to gather their wits, their gear, and to flee: "Hurry, I cannot hold him forever. Meglog is too strong. Quickly, you have to escape this fissure, while you can."

As the whispering wind moved through the company, the soldiers turned to observe that Meglog was immobilized. The creature stood, like a giant gargoyle, frozen in place.

The army sensed their time of escape had come. The troops rushed to gather whatever supplies and equipment they could cart before they ran from the passage. They marched for almost a pace-stay. Tired, hungry, and grief-stricken the soldiers dared not to halt until they cleared the canyon.

After another half a pace-stay march, they exited the gorge, and still the company trudged onward until fatigue overtook them, and they required rest.

"Company halt," ordered Captain Gareth.

"Lieutenant, have the men break in to their squads. Set a rotating watch on the outer parameter while the remainder of the men rest, and have all the officers met me at my camp in ten arcs. I will go and address the men, and then we shall convene."

"Yes, sir," replied Lieutenant Cartwright.

"The loss of Lord Hamilton decrees that I assume command of this company. He gave his life so that we could escape to fight another day. I know you are tired. We will rest and eat in due course. The rest will be short, as we must leave come morn because we still must get to Ganoll in two pace-stays. All of Lendaw is counting on us achieving our mission. Let us not fail in our duty to defend the rights and freedoms of those who cannot fight. Let us fight in the name of liberty. Let us fight to keep Lendaw free from totalitarianism and oppression. Are you with me?"

"Aye," roared the company in unison.

"Then take rest and food. We leave at first light," commanded Cartwright.

CHAPTER 12

Lost

As they journeyed to Oildale, a small trading post beside the Kuggar River, near the Twin Mountains, and just west of Mudluck, Jenna and Cáel quietly chatted amongst themselves. She mentioned that, at school, she was somewhat of a bookworm and that she spent most of her time studying. She explained that, when not in school, she worked part-time.

Cáel asked about Earth.

Jenna attempted to describe great cities with hundreds of thousands of people. She told of skyscrapers, buildings, and houses. She described trains, buses, automobiles, and trucks that drove along many highways, bi-ways and road. She talked of the issues affecting the planet: The contrast between the rich and the poor, those who worked and those unemployed, she spoke of pollution, famine and disasters. She expressed her hope that people would one day figure it all out somehow.

Cáel tried to understand. Try as he might, he could never picture such a world, and he stated as such to Jenna. Jenna laughed and she promised him that when this, waving her arms about her, was over; she would show him her world.

Jenna was very happy. She had met a man who made her feel wonderful. He made her laugh, he was patient with her while they trained together, and he accepted her for who she was quirks and all. She liked him too. He was tall, handsome, and brave; she liked confidence and that he humble about it. He could admit that he was wrong or that he did not know something. He loved her, she knew and she loved him she realized. She could picture the two of them making a life together.

She smiled at Cáel. He looked at her and asked, "What?"

"Nothing, I just wanted to tell you that I love you."

Cryall held up her arm to get them to hush. She whispered to them, "I heard something."

They all stood still and listened for any strange sounds. After a few moments, they resumed their journey. The enemy swiftly ambushed them. The little group was hopelessly out numbered. "Everyone quick, run!" yelled Alistair as he cast a spell to prevent capture. They each raced in a different direction and each hoped to evade apprehension.

While they all managed to escape, they sensed a trap. Their adversary herded them in an eastward direction. Try as they might, the heroes were cutoff in every other direction. No matter which direction they chose, they were each force east. Still there was no other alternative. They were hopelessly out numbered.

Dagin, I should have planned this out better. There is nothing to it. I can only hope for a means of escape ahead. I simply cannot not possible fight off an army with my spells that would leave me defenseless. I should have planned our next move better.

"Up ahead there was a cave, quick everyone in there," indicated Alistair while he pointed to the cave entrance ahead. The others gave Alistair a look as if to say, "Frag it." They each sensed danger. Nonetheless, there was no other option. They fled into the cave. Alistair casted a spell to delay their followers and exclaimed, "That will hold them for a while."

"Where to now?" asked Cryall.

"Down this way," he stated as he pointed to the chamber on the left while igniting his staff with a white-bluish light.

Almost at once, Alistair regretted his decision. Instead of staying along the perimeter of the cave, as he had hoped, the pathway started to descend and downward the little group raced. Deeper and deeper they travelled and then the path gradually leveled off and went to the right.

Eventually, the group came to an entry of a huge chamber with a giant fissure. The abyss appeared to drop into nothingness. To the naked eye, it seemed bottomless. The only passage was a rock bridge at the other end of the cavern.

Jenna followed Alistair who was in the lead. Cáel and Cryall trailed close behind. The companions heard the stomps of the approaching troops. They picked up their pace. As Alistair and Jenna cleared the cross, there was a huge explosion. Jenna gazed back, in time, to witness Cáel and Cryall fall from the edge and into the abyss.

Everything went into slow motion.

"No-o-o-o-o-o," Jenna raged, releasing a surge of magical energy directly at the enemy entering the cavern. The blast tore at the emerging soldiers ripping them to shreds. The entrance to the chamber rattled and rumbled until the entry was shattered and blocked with rubble. She could no longer stand. She crumbled to the ground like the rock before her mumbling, "No, no, it can't be. Say it isn't so," sobbed Jenna. Jenna was in shock.

Alistair sensing there was still danger, tried to coax her to her feet saying, "Jenna dear, we are not safe here we must get going," gently prodding her to stand. Jenna rose hesitantly to her feet. Alistair led her forward through the only path before them.

Jenna was able to move. She walked as if her legs were lead. Each step forward required effort until her legs began to shake and stiffen. She was very cold and the chill reached to her bones. She had no sense where Alistair was leading her, nor did she care. To her, everything seemed hazy.

She had lost the love of her life and a good friend. The love and care they showed for her, she never experienced before. At school and at work she had friends who were nothing more than that. They were not close. At home, it was just her and the Humes and their love was unconditional.

Jenna never felt alone as she did at this moment.

After a little while, Alistair discovered a small grotto and the two settled there.

"Jenna you need nourishment and rest. Here Jenna have some of this. It will help you gain your strength and help you to rest."

"What is it?"

"It is Theriac a healing elixir. A fair warning, it tastes awful. It is best you just swallow it down."

Jenna did as Alistair requested and immediately she felt better. She was still tired and laid down to rest. Jenna slept for six arcs and when she awoke, she felt refreshed, warmth, and comforted.

"Ah, I see you are awake," exclaimed Alistair, "How are you feeling? You must be famished. Here eat some of this," stated Alistair and handed her some food from his travelling pouch.

"I don't know where to begin," Jenna sobbed. "It's all surreal. I can't believe I have lost the man I love and my good friend."

Jenna and Alistair continued to sit to discuss the past events.

After about an arc when Jenna had cried herself out, Alistair stated, "We must get moving soon. We cannot risk staying here much longer."

"I know. One-half of me wallows in grief and cannot continue, while the other half realizes that if I do not move, then I may be the next to die. I don't want to die," she paused, "I think you are right, we must get moving."

"That's my girl," he stated encouragingly, as he helped her to her feet and patted her back tenderly.

The two gathered their belongings and continued the journey down the tunnel. They travelled for a long time until the came to a fork.

"Left or Right?" asked Alistair.

"Well, we went left last time and that choice didn't go well perhaps we should try right," stated Jenna tentatively.

"Very well, that sounds as good as any direction to go."

The pair travelled hesitantly down the tunnel. The slope was heading upward which gave the two hopes that they would soon escape the confinement of their enclosure, which was getting tiresome for them both.

As they continued their ascent, they saw the opening ahead. *They would soon be free.*

When Jenna and Alistair exited the cavern, all hell broke loose.

Anko, the Shadeen, and a hoard of soldiers were waiting. Before either Alistair or Jenna could react, Anko casted a knock out spell rendering both of them unconscious. When Alistair awoke, Jenna and the Uglandan were gone.

CHAPTER 13

Muwtag

Jenna awoke with a start, "Alistair," she implored? There was no reply.

The nightmare she awoke from was a review of the last few hours of Cáel and Cryall falling into the void.

She found herself on the floor, which was cold and damp. She sat up. *Where am I? What is this place? Where's Alistair?*

It was dark. Jenna casted the incantation, "Illuminavit," just as Alistair had shown her. The spell failed.

What's wrong? Why didn't the spell work?

She attempted several other spells yet they too were unsuccessful. She started to fret that she lost her powers.

Oh God, let it not be so.

It took a many more moments, and once Jenna regained her composure, she began to examine the room. The room was cold. It numbed her fingers and toes. Bone chilling as it was, it was tolerable. The room was dark. She could not make out any forms or shadows and there was no hint of light anywhere in the room. The stench of the air was obvious. It smelt of rotted garbage. She heard scratching and scraping sounds within the room. Try as she might, Jenna could not determine from whence the noise came. She extended her arms and using her hands felt the items in front of her. After a while, she determined that she was in some type of cell. The room was approximately a hundred square feet in area. It contained a bed-size stone bench opposite the sealed door.

Jenna paced back and forth. She tried to make sense of everything: how did she get here and why? Jenna pondered her predicament. Frustrated, she concluded nothing made any sense.

At first, she had pleaded for release. After many failed attempts, she gave up. She was a prisoner.

Jenna sat curled up at the top corner of the bench where she discovered a blanket. She wrapped the tattered blanket around her, hugged her knees and began to rock herself. For the first time in a while, she was petrified of what might to happen to her. She was glad for the blanket. It provided her some small comfort.

Her captures slipped her meals through a slot at the bottom of the door. Jenna knew she would have to keep her strength if she had any hope of survival. She ate the tasteless food.

Without a point of reference, it was hard for Jenna to know day from night and vice-versa. Time blurred. Jenna could no longer determine the length of her incarceration. She began to despair.

Jenna feared to sleep. Rest brought the nightmares: first Danyll dying, then Gnoz missing and next Cáel and Cryall are falling. Each dream became more intense – the fall, the deaths, the screams jolted her from sleep. Jenna was panic-stricken. She was both: too afraid of sleep and she too tired to keep awake. She did not know how much longer she could endure this torture.

Just when her torment became too much and she could take no more, the door opened.

"The Master will see you now," sneered the ogre that opened the door.

The guard guided her through the many, and poorly, lit passages of the dungeon. Gradually, they reached the upper castle corridors. Jenna shielded her eyes from the light of the lantern. The two moved further along the corridors of castle. Jenna felt trapped like a mouse within a maze. Around and around the moved until the pathway opened into a great hall. The guard rapped on the door.

"Enter."

"Your Lordship," stated the guard who bowed slightly.

"Ah, I see you have brought our guest. Welcome," smiled Anko.

Jenna entered the chamber.

She stood and observed the man who stood before her: He appeared to be about five foot and ten inches in height, he weighed about one hundred and fifty-five pounds, and he was about fifty years of age. He had a short salt and peppered colored beard with mid-length hair. He wore a brown riding outfit and boots, and he carried a grey and black staff adorned with a green stone on top.

She was unsure how to proceed and she opted to remain put.

"I must apologize for my bad manners." He turned and walked to the far end of a large table. "You were suppose be a guess and you were to be given all the honors in accordance."

All my plans ruined. These blasted idiots nearly ruined it all. They imprisoned her when I specifically instructed them to treat her as my guest. I wanted them to house her in the guest quarters of the castle. The castle was a pretense whose only purpose was to make Ugland appear to be a just and civil society. Their error may have cost me my plans. I need to win the girl over – to woo her into joining forces with me. Together Jenna and I would rule the world. Perhaps I can still persuade her to my side.

Jenna stood silently.

"I was away, so I could not make arrangements myself. Once I heard that you were in the dungeons, I had you sent for immediately."

Seeing Jenna's hesitation, Anko beckoned her to sit at the table. "Please have a seat, dear. I am Anko, Lord of Ugland and you are Jenna of the Weir. Are you not?"

The guard gently nudged Jenna forward. Jenna took the hint and she stepped forward. Once she reached the large table, she sat down at the opposite end and replied, "Yes."

"I have ordered a feast for us to feed on. I do believe you will find it most enjoyable. We can become better acquainted over the course meal," smiled Anko.

"May I ask some questions?"

"Of course my dear, please, do make your-self at home. Ask away," stated Anko as he gestured for Jenna to speak.

"Where am I and how did I get here?"

"Ah, you are in Muwtag a small city in the very south-east of Ugland. As I have just explained, I have invited you. You are my guest here."

The food began to arrive. The platters of meats and fresh vegetables filled the table and flasks of Kaidesh and a bowl of Clasa, a fruit wine found only in Ugland, were set.

Jenna was unsure as to how to proceed.

She knew that she was no more a guest than Gnoz who was likewise a prisoner here at Muwtag. The pits must be nearby. I must play the part and bide my time.

"One more question if I may," continued Jenna cautiously.

"Where are my things? I seemed to have lost my rucksack and my weapons."

"I am unsure of their whereabouts. I will have my people investigate for you. Now please enough of these questions. Let us eat, drink, and get merry. I very much would like us to be friends."

The meal was ample at best. Anko and Jenna traded small talk of their experiences and travels. Over time, Jenna began to reveal more details of life. She was unaware she was so talkative. She became increasingly chatty.

She was unstoppable until it dawned on her what she was doing. It was then she realized her error.

Anko drugged her food. She laid her utensils upon the table and she stopped eating and drinking.

Anko kept probing her for information.

As difficult as it was, she knew that she had to keep her replies cryptic and to keep her answers brief. She explained that she was from Terra and that her father was from Lendaw. She continued by stating she had come to Lendaw at Alistair's request to take her rightful place as heir.

By meals end, Jenna feared she revealed too much information. The drug, by this time, was wearing off. Jenna quickly rehearsed the evening's events in her head and she concluded that she revealed no pertinent information. She persuaded herself that Anko acquired no information that he did already possess.

"I have arranged quarters for you. You are free to travel throughout the castle. For your protection, I have arranged an armed escort at all times. These are perilous times with troop movement from the north."

The two departed their separate ways.

The escort led Jenna to a small room in the eastern tower of the castle. Jenna's assigned room was scarcely furnished still it was better than the cell that previously imprisoned her. It had a water basin and a proper bed for which she graciously used.

Jenna refrained from eating or drinking anything that her captives provided for her consumption. She disposed of them down the garderobe, which emptied into the moat surrounding the castle. Jenna wondered how much longer she could continue this ruse. She was able to acquire water on her trips on her walks throughout the castle. Still, it was difficult to get food. The few scraps of food that she managed to acquire would not sustain her for long.

As the days passed, Jenna began to feel clearheaded. Her dreams were less intense. She managed to casts several small spells. They were intermittent. She worried about the inconsistency sometimes they work and other times not so much. She reasoned that there was still some trace of the drugs in her system.

Every day the soldiers she reported to Anko. He continued to probe for information and each day she managed to defer his interrogations. This was not as difficult as it seemed. The Aryan Council excluded her from most discussions of troop numbers, movements or general planning from her.

Jenna succeeded to avert any discussion as to why she came to Lendaw. She evaded most of his enquiries. She found this more and more difficult to do with each meeting.

After four days, a guard summoned her to appear before Anko. If there was a pretense on their first meeting, then there was none today.

"Ah Jenna, I have summoned you because I have questions that need answers."

Anko drilled her for information, and at every opportunity, she tried to evade a direct response. Jenna witnessed the frustration in his face.

Anko raged, "I tire of this game. I know why you came to Lendaw. I know that Alistair has plans for you. I know you have magic. I know the magic is strong with you. Do not take me for a fool. I will get the information I require one way or another, but first, I will have that trinket you wear so fondly."

Before Jenna could react, Anko grasped the amulet in his hand.

"You supposed that I had not observed you desperately clinging to this ornament like a talisman. You are mistaken. Your actions betray you. It must have great meaning for you to cherish it so. I think I will keep it to learn of its secrets."

Jenna felt utterly hopeless without the Iluminar. She felt useless. The Iluminar was gone and there was no way to retrieve it. She was defenseless.

"Take her to the pits," he ordered, "Perhaps then, she will be more co-operative."

The Pits consisted of three mining pits and one used for captives. It was the former, which they transferred Jenna. This specific pit served as Anko's lair. It was here that Anko practiced the dark craft.

CHAPTER 14

Survivors

"Crom would say that Durkin had lost touch with reality," or so Bilpin reasoned. He could not believe that there could be survivors at Lagr Gardr yet Durkin held the axe in his hand, so he had to believe the rest of Durkin's tale.

They came to seek the very weapon that Durkin now possessed. How was he to deny what he beheld with his very eyes? Durkin possessed the Mjolnir. How could he now to dismiss what was real? Was he so jealous of his brother's gift? Perhaps when he first began this quest, he hoped he would be the chosen one. Now that he was not, was he now envious of Durkin?

Bilpin shook his head, no.

He had no option than to support his brother whatever came.

If Durkin's initial estimates were correct, then they were nearing the fortress.

Why Elek left the safety of the fortress that day he would never really know. He had a feeling that he could not shake. Young Terk begged him to come and Elek obliged. He knew that he should not concede to his nephew's wishes. If he was not careful, then he would spoil the boy and that would be a dangerous thing to do. Especially, since they were refugees and their people had limited supplies. As if sensing danger, Elek turned to his nephew, "Go inside little one. This is no place for you. It is not safe for you here," stated Elek, solemnly.

Nor, anyone for that matter.

Five cycles, that was how long they had sought refuge here at Lagr Gardr or "Little Dwelling". One of, if not, the smallest stronghold the dwarves had. It was located at the furthest north-west crest corner of the Andar Mountains. It was a perilous journey. Some of their members never survived the trip and they perished along the way. Many opted to stay behind, namely, the old, the frail, and those with very young ones. They chose to risk taking shelter in nearby forts. He feared for their lives.

Griminar protect them.

He shook his head, "No." He no longer believed in a god that would suffer his people thusly; nonetheless, he offered the prayer just the same.

Elek was about to turn into the fortress, as he started to go, he heard a sound behind him. Elek raised he weapon and spun around. "Halt, who goes there?"

"Ellri", the voice replied.

Elek did not know whether to laugh or cry. He could not believe his ears. There was only one person who ever called him that.

"Hiyo, Durkin. I assumed you were dead."

"You can't rid of me that easily Ellri," as the two embraced.

"Hiyo, Bilpin," stated Elek, as they clasped at mid arms.

He was never so happy to see two people in all his life.

"This is a joy! Welcome, now hurry along before someone discovers us."

Elek led the two into the cavern. As the two brothers reached for the lanterns nearby, Elek sealed the opening with a stone. If they had not passed this way, then they would never know a doorway existed here. The seal was that good. There did not appear to be a seam anywhere along the wall they just passed through. As if sensing his question, Elek replied, "It is old magic. A subtle spell casted by Nephric the old cleric, it is supposed to be undetectable by enchanters and the Shadeen."

The three travelled through the many passages until the came upon a courtyard. It was as if they had not travelled through a network of caves and passageways. The sky, it was unbelievable. Open air.

"Nye, your eyes are not betraying you. Lagr Gardr the smallest of our hamlets, yet it is one of the most spectacular to behold. I would not believe it either, myself, if I had not seen it with my own eyes.

"Who knew such a place existed?" Bilpin and Durkin stood with the open in awe.

The hold was small of that there was no doubt. The fortress consisted of a large courtyard surrounded by housing and nothing further.

"There is nothing beyond the buildings you see before you except the cliff edge. The drop appears to continue forever. It drops further than anything I ever saw before," stated Elek simply.

They walked by the furthest buildings and sure enough except for a gap for walking and some gardening behind the houses, the homestead ended at the wall with a large drop.

"Aren't you afraid the children might scale the wall and fall," asked Bilpin?

Elek picked up a rock from the ground and he threw it. As the rock climbed higher and it soared toward the wall, it hit something and it stopped in mid-air.

Bilpin looked bewildered.

"It is some kind of field. Nothing can pass it and trust me; the children have tried."

"How can all this be? The open space, and the force field, how can they be? Tell me, have these items existed before? If they had, surely our people would have known about them beforehand."

"I am not sure. One would think this," pointing around, "would be well known. No one here has ever seen the likes of it. Most of our people have never been to Lagr Gardr beforehand. They believed it to be too insignificant because of its small size. I think they were wrong." Elek paused, and then he continued, "Of those who settled here, their elders stated that they happened upon this place by accident and when they realized its potential, they decided to stay remain. There is an ancient scroll, which none here can fully decipher. What little information that they did decipher, hints that this fortress has been here since the beginning of Dwarven existence. The housing is dwarfish in nature. No other race could live here. Whoever, or whatever, created this place; it was meant for our people."

"How many, how many of our people survived," asked Durkin tentatively?

"There are approximately ten thousand of us. Of that number, a nearly quarter is elderly or children."

"Sigh, what has happen since Bilpin and I left? We have things to tell. First, I need to know what happened to our people."

"We saw the armies approach of course. Their numbers filled the Andar plain. The giants, the ogres and the trolls marched through the plain and up the mountain passes. By this time, most of the old, women and children had already fed the city for the safety of the outer edged strongholds. The enemy attacked the outlining towns and cities, and then Gunnik itself. They were merciless in their attack. The giants, ogres and trolls murdered all who got in their way. They indiscriminately massacred all who stood in their way whether that person was man, woman, and child, or whether they were old or young. It was a hopeless situation. We were greatly outnumbered. Yet, we fought back bravely. No matter how we hard we fought, the enemy continued to strike us down as easily as axes to trees. In the latter parts of the battle, your father ordered a half of the troops and I to retrieve, and to take the remaining civilians to safety. We went northwestward to seek shelter. We met others groups along the way and we joined forces with them. We continued northwestward. I managed to convince the survivors that Lagr Gardr was our only hope. I read the stories and I heard the legions. The path was difficult and perilous. Some people did not survive the journey."

Elek paused, "There is one more thing: Tharin fell in battle. I saw it with my own eyes. I am sorry to be the one to tell you. I know he was your father."

For the brothers, this was the saddest news. Their King, and father, was dead.

"That makes me King," mourned Bilpin.

That I am King should be a joyous occasion, yet it is not I cannot. Now is not the time for celebration. Our loss is too great. I am heart-broken-hearted, first our people; now our father and our king. Perhaps there will come a time when we can celebrate. This is not that day.

"Elek, summon the elders and the troops in the great hall," pointing to his left, "there is much to discuss and to plan. My brother and I need a few moments to collect ourselves."

"Don't say it Bilpin. It will not do to play 'what-ifs'. Things are what they are. We both know that this was bound to happen one day. We cannot be in two places at the same time. If we had stayed, then we would likely both be dead. No, events occur for a reason. If we had not left, then you would not be holding the Mjolnir now."

"I cannot argue with you there. I just wish."

"I hear you brother and I share your sentiment. I wish I could talk with him again too. Let's go and get this over with, so we can finally get some rest."

The elders met with the two brothers late into the night. The brothers recapped their journey to Alyra. They told of the Weir family return to the land in the form of a young female named Jenna, and how the Slavidian threaten to take revenge on her. They explained that the Assembly learned of troop movements in the southeast, and the attack on the dwarves. They reiterated how the two brothers sought to return home to offer whatever assistance that was required. They concluded with the story of the battle with Cocidius at Haugr Passage and the procurement of the Mjolnir and Odinson's charge to find the dwarf survivors.

"Now that we are all up-to-date on current affairs, we need to discuss our current state of previsions and manpower. Darmak, what is the status of our provisions and what is the state of our army?"

"My Lord, we have ample food and shelter. We require greater numbers of fighters and weapons. There are approximately ten thousand souls. A third of that number includes those men of age or those near of age, which are ready for battle. If we include the women folk, then we could bring that number to nearly fifty percent. As for armory, we are unsure. We have yet to search all the stores of the fortress. The stronghold has numerous small chambers below. They still require searching. Since the settlement is small, we believe it is unlikely to have a large cache in its armory."

"Then a thorough search of the lower chambers must be our first priority, and an inventory must be made of all rations and weaponry. We must conduct a censuses of every man, woman and child residing here. We need a better count of those residing here. I will leave the details to you Darmak since you are the elder of Lagr Gardr. Until the surveys are complete, we will call this meeting to an end. We will meet in a few days to plan our next move."

Elek suggested that they call it a night and get some rest.

Durkin and Bilpin declined the offer of the most luxurious quarters in the complex. They chose to camp in the common hall where most of the settlement inhabited, and they opted for a spot in one of the corners. They lit a tiny fire, and bed down to sleep. When the brothers awoke, it was late afternoon.

After a quick meal, the brothers decided to explore the stronghold further. As they moved through the complex, Bilpin observed the sorry state that was the dwarf existence. As if sensing their thoughts, Elek stated simply, "We have attempted to shelter the people. Most of them opted to live in the hallways instead. When so much has been lost, one cannot feel worthy of any comfort that life may provide. It is enough to have food, clothing and shelter. I think it was the same with you two last night."

The sorry state of the dwarves, that was an understatement when one considered the reality of the current situation. People sat scattered throughout the complex with little or no possessions. Most of the then looked ragged, tired and defeated. Their very nature was changed. There was no joy and happiness found in any of the faces of those they saw.

In utter angst Bilpin fumed, "No more!" He continued, "Since the dawn of time when Griminar molded the dwarves from the clay of Andar, our people flourished. We grew as a people. We created the great cities of Gunnik, Therin, Cobnr, and Genae. During the Orkan War when our people were nearly defeated, Griminar sent us our deliverer in the person of Odinson who yielded the mighty Mjolnir to strike down our enemies. We did not just take refuge and we hide. Nae, more than that we prospered until we grew in number and in strength. Over time, we grew complacent and weak. We opted to isolate ourselves and to severe, all ties with our allies. That we abandoned our friends was probably shortsighted. We supposed ourselves to be invincible. Today we humbly stand and we are near extinction. True as these facts may be, I am here to assure you that we will rebuild. My brother found what was once lost to us: 'the Hammer of Strength' and through it we have hope. By Griminar's grace, our people will survive and flourish. Nae, more than that, today I swear to you as your King and Protector that we will thrive. Our number will grow in magnitude as stars in the night sky. We will avenge our dead, we will strike fear in the hearts of our enemies, and we will crush the bones of any, and all, those who would dare oppose us."

CHAPTER 15

MarGraven

MarGraven was depressing. It was the bleakest place that Jenna had ever seen. Even before Jenna entered its eerie tentacles, the dismal, chard and shadowy remains of the landscape sent shivers down her spine. For miles, Jenna observed neither vegetation nor any signs of life upon the surface of earth. If Jenna believed that the surface was bad, then she was greatly mistaken. Upon entering the adit leading to the lower shafts of the pit, the first thing she noticed was the stench of the place. The pungent odor of death and decay filled the entire cavern. Jenna gagged with each breathe she took. Her sheer willpower prevented her from getting sick. The second item she noticed was the sorry state of those in the chain gangs she saw upon her travels. She came to realize that the images of the filthy, poor, and emaciated figures working the mines was nothing to the fact that the greater horror was they resembled nothing more than walking zombies.

Her captures took her to a cell in the lower chambers of the pits. Her cell was damp and cold. There was nothing. Only darkness filled the room except for the miniscule amount of greenish light emitted at the base of the door.

 The horror of MarGraven paled in comparison to the panic that Jenna found herself in without the comfort of the Iluminar under her shirt. For the first time in quite a while, Jenna was at a lost for what to do. Disheartened Jenna curled herself upon the bench within her cell and rocked back and forth.

After a few hours in her cell, Jenna attempted a number of small spells without success. She feared that without the amulet, she would never perform magic again. She felt defenseless without it. Jenna grew more concerned about her predicament.

Whenever there were footsteps outside her door, Jenna panicked with fright. She feared for her safety and her future. Try as she might to stay calm, she could not stop imagining the worst that could happen. Jenna fretted about her future until the point she was near exhaustion. When she dozed off, sleep provided little rest. Her sleep was full of nightmare scenarios. She dreamt of the death of Danyll, the capture of Gnoz, her capture and imprisonment. The worst of it was her reliving the deaths of Cryall and Cáel. She snapped awaked whenever she relived their fall. It was then that she realized she was truly alone.

This was most disturbing for her.

The hours turned into days, and the days turned to weeks. Time had no meaning in this place and Jenna was clueless as to the duration of her imprisonment. It seemed to her to be months.

The others must believe I am dead.

Despite her hunger and thirst, her paranoia prevented her from taking any food or drink presented to her. The food and drink her captures provided through the clasped hatch in the door laid untouched. After Jenna's last experience, she did not trust her captures not to drug the food and drink presented to her. Without her magic, Jenna needed all her wits about her.

"Wham, Wham, Wham," Jenna covered her ears.

Please God, not again. I don't know how much more I can take.

Since her imprisonment, the sound was constant. She did not know its source, nor did she wish to know. She avoided all speculation as to what it could be. She was afraid. All she knew was that the sound was starting to get on her nerves, and that if it continued, then eventually she would go insane.

Time crept slowly forward. Jenna sat on the bench until she could sit no more. She rose and paced the length of her cell – back and forth, she paced until she became bored. She decided to sleep. She lay down on the bench where she tossed and turned for hours on end. When sleep failed her, she sat up again.

No matter what she tried, she could not prevent herself from the worry of what terrors the future held. It was useless. Jenna sighed. She discovered that she could no longer fret about events that may, or may not occur. She decided to face the unknown with strength and dignity. The worst that could happen was her death, and if that was her fate, then so be it.

Jenna turned to the bench and sat down. She crossed her legs and started practicing the meditative exercises of Teleclero. When Cryall first taught her the Hatha Exercises of Teleclero, she thought that they were a waste of time. Now she found that the exercises soothing and they helped her to center herself.

The cell door opened. Her guards gestured her to follow them, she did so willingly, and without hesitation.

"Ah, there you are. I heard you have not been eating or drinking. I assure you that if I wanted you dead, then I would have had you executed and be done with it, or are you afraid your nourishment is drugged? If you are, then I assure you, I have better means of making you more co-operative. No, I only wish to show you my lair and the gifts that it promises. If history is any indication, Alistair can be so restrictive with his apprentice. I was once his apprentice that was before I discovered the power of Vis Colli, the Dark Magic, as practiced by my late master Urian. It is a power unlike anything one can experience. I offer its magic as a gift to you. I do not wish for us to be enemies. No matter what propaganda they sold you, I am not the monster they portrayed me to be."

"If that is so, then why am I imprisoned here?"

"I just wanted to show you the realities of life here on Lendaw. There is a philosophical divide as to the nature and practice of magic. Vis Colli gets its energy from Ka, or the life force of all living things. We necromancers wield Ka to form magic. Over the centuries, the debated continued as to which form of Magic offers the true path. I believe the practice of Vis Colli is the path to true enlightenment. Alistair and the elves have opposing beliefs. They believe the practice Vis Colli to be dangerous to Lendaw and to oneself. I believe they err on the side of caution. I believe Vis Colli to be the true source of power and strength. You have only seen one side. I wish to show you the other. Let us take a walk shall we?"

Anko lead Jenna down through to the inner sanctum of the lair. The whooping sound that Jenna heard earlier was getting louder and louder as the two neared their destination.

The lair was a multi-layered chamber that resembled some the pictures of the catacombs of Ancient Greece and Rome she saw on National Geographic.

Oh god, this is when I discover the source of the whooping sound. I am not sure I want to know.

Jenna kept her best poker face as she continued downward through the chamber. She followed Anko into a vault where she saw a large red stone dais in the center of the chamber. The bloodstone platform was the source of power for Vis Colli from it the necromancer practiced the dark arts. Anko stood upon the dais and summoned the magic. Such was the power of Vis Colli, its strength caused the room to shake and thunder unlike anything Jenna experienced before. Jenna observed how the magic affected him strangely. The dark magic caused Anko became ecstatic and he lost all sense of self. He surrendered himself to its currents and intimacies. For Jenna though, the effect of the dark magic was the opposite upon her. Its aura made her nauseous. Every fiber of her being opposed its draw. She became dizzy. She almost passed out. With the last of her strength, Jenna fled the chamber.

Unsure of her path, Jenna travelled deeper and deeper into the sanctuary. The whooping sound intensified as she approached nearer and nearer to its source of which she was immediately, horrified to discover as she entered the atrium was a crushing machine that crushed anything beneath its workings.

The creatures were led to the entrance of the machine were zombie-like. Like sheep toward the slaughter. The failed to see what was to befall them. Each entered the mechanism never to return. The drop hammer smashed its victims to their deaths and their remnants gathered in the vat below.

Horrified by what she witnessed, Jenna turned her face away.

A little while later Anko rushed into the room with two guards.

Jenna faced him. "You want me to be a part of this?" She shrieked in disgust.

"I had hoped you wouldn't witness this rite. As terrible as it seems, the sacrifice of a life is necessary. The life force is the basis of Vis Colli. Do not be so rash to judge. I do them a great service. Now their deaths have meaning. They provide me with the magic that I so greatly desire. The victims old and decrepit. Besides, they feel nothing. It is a quick and painless way to die and," he paused, "everything has its time and everyone dies."

Jenna stormed from the room and she began to gag. When the gagging subsided, she stood up. Anko came and he stood beside her.

"If that is the cost of power, then I want no part of it. I will never be a part of something which requires death to achieve its gains."

"You do not know the power of the dark arts. It is a power such that you can only imagine, and with it, one can conquer worlds."

Jenna stood defiantly in front of Anko.

"If you do not join me, then you too shall die. Take her back to her cell."

The guards escorted Jenna back to her cell. Jenna she curled herself upon the bench. She rocked herself back and forth. No matter what she tried to distract her thoughts of the images she witnessed, she could not block the horrors from her mind. She now understood why no one ever returned from MarGraven. She wondered if Gnoz faced this fate. She immediately regretted thinking such a thing as the thought saddened her terribly.

Jenna went on another hunger strike. She believed any food and drink they offered to be tainted. The days passed. Her stomached ached and rumbled with hunger pains and she was very thirsty. Only the Hatha Exercises prevented her from giving in to her craving for food and water. Jenna wondered how long she could continue her act of defiance. She shook her head. She had no inkling.

Within a few more days, she had her answer. She must drink. Her mouth was parched and she grew weak and dizzy. She could not hold off any longer. She reached for the glass and swallowed its contents. She did not give it a second thought until later.

If they drugged it, then it was a risk that she had to take. She could no longer continue without water.

The little food and water she risked to consume did little to strengthen or sustain her. She began to grow sick with a fever. Something was wrong. Jenna was unable to determine what that was, or why she was getting sick. She only knew that if she did not get out, then she would die here. One way or another, she would die.

CHAPTER 16

Escape

"Jenna, get up."

The ape-like and melanin-less creature standing before her looked like one of the creatures of the book The Time Machine by H. G. Wells called a Morlock. At first, Jenna thought she was dreaming then the creature spoke her name again something she thought Morlocks were incapable of doing.

"Who are you?"

"No time for that now. We have little time in which to make our escape."

"That voice, I have heard it before."

"Yes, I have no time to explain. You must drink this and come with me," stated the Morlock holding a flask.

"How do I know, that the drink is not poison or something?"

The Morlock uncorked the flask and took a swift of the drink. "Are you satisfied? We are running out of time. You must make up your mind quickly. Do you want to get out of here or do you wish to remain?"

Jenna sensed that this was not the time to debate. She took the flask and gulped down its contents, "Augh, that tasted horrible, what was that stuff?"

"It was a mixture of Theriac and Canese. The use of Theriac is for healing and the Canese shields the mind. With their use, I can shield you and we can make our escape. Come, follow me and do not speak under any circumstances, do you understand?"

Jenna nodded and followed the Morlock out of her cell. As she departed, she noted the two Morlocks unconscious outside her cell.

"We go up from here."

They traversed the well-guarded corridors as if unseen. The Morlock and Jenna weaved through the passages and ascended ever upwards. As the neared the adit, Jenna heard a voice in her head, "We come to the perilous part of our journey, stay close to me and try not to make a sound. If anyone tries to stop us, pretend that you are my prisoner."

As the exited the mine, Jenna noted that it dawn and the Morlock was gone and an Imperial Sentry stood in its place. In shock, Jenna almost let out a squeal.

The two marched the open face of the mine when the Sentries patrolling the outer ridges of the mine quickly intercepted them, "Halt, who goes there?"

"Do you not recognize an Imperial Guard when you see one?"

"We have orders to detain all who enter, or exit MarGraven."

"I am sure that your orders do not include the Imperial staff. If you doubt this, you are unwise. Do you wish to test me? It would be in your best interest to obey my orders, or you will never see sunlight again."

The two sentries looked at each other unsure as to how to act.

"I have orders to take this prisoner to Muwtag as Anko's concubine. We require horse and carriage. She is Felaga Adr, First Wife. You treat her with the courtesy deserved her."

The waited tensely as the guards left to retrieve two horses and a buggy. Jenna began to worry that the gig was up. Finally, the sentries presented the coach. Jenna climbed into the carriage while the Imperial Guard mounted the driver's seat. When both of them settled in, they slowly drove off. Kate changed her route to a northward direction and sped away after they were out of sight of the mine until they were a pace-stay away.

"Jenna, this is where we get off."

Jenna stepped out from the carriage and was surprise to see Lady Hamilton sitting in the driver's seat.

"Lady Hamilton!"

"Please, call me Kate," she stated with a smile. "This is no time for formalities. We must be at Erenhil in four pace-stays and we do not have much time. We took longer to get away than I thought we would. Help me unhitch the horses. The carriage will only slow us down and by now they will know that we have made our escape."

"But…"

"No time for questions, like you, I am not of Lendaw. I am the sole survivor of my race the 'Xxyrlos'. I arrived in Lendaw through the Portal like you. A great war tore open a fabric of space-time between the worlds and I made my escape through it. Alistair rescued me. He took me to Alyra where he nursed me back to health. I am humanoid. I am neither human nor Lendawan. I have the ability to shield objects and people, and to make them appear to be whatever I will them to be. This is how I managed to get you out."

Jenna stunned by this news exclaimed, "Umm, you're so Alyran, with all their pomp and circumstance."

"It was all an act. It is all too stuffy for my taste. My marrying Charles changed all that; his title demanded that I adopt Alyran norms."

Jenna felt dizzy and tired. She collapsed into to Kate's arms. Kate managed to prevent her fall to the ground.

"You are still too weak the Theriac should have lasted much, much longer. Here have some more." Kate took another flask out and handed it to Jenna, which Jenna drink thankfully. After a few moments, Jenna felt renewed energy and strength.

"Are you able to ride or shall we ride together?"

"I think I can manage," she stuttered.

"We ride to Erenhil; home of the elves. Even by horse, it is still difficult journey. Let me know when you tire and we will rest for a bit."

The women travelled quickly through the landscape. Occasionally, they stopped to rest. Jenna grilled for updates on current events. Kate avoided all her enquiries. She explained that it was unsafe to discuss anything so far from the protection of Erenhil.

The two women passed through the outskirts of Ligwick. Enemy forces scattered the land. Kate and Jenna skirted the land and backed tracked their journey every once. They chose to prod onward and to rest near Tepic as it was nearer to the safety of Erenhil.

While Jenna slept, Kate stood guard.

"They would reach Tepic by the morning," and this thought made Kate very pleased. From there they would reach Erenhil within two pace-stays. They were far from safe and danger lurched at every turn.

Kate heard murmurs. She went back to the small fire. She looked down on the sleeping girl. Jenna's sleep was restless. She moaned and tossed in her sleep. Kate shook her awake.

"Are you okay?"

"It was just a nightmare. How long was I asleep?"

"Not long, maybe we should continue onward."

CHAPTER 17

Erenhil

Kate grew concerned for Jenna. Since Jenna last woke up, she grew weaker by the moment. Whatever the spell Jenna was under, it was a powerful one, for no amount of the elixir was effective against it. Jenna weakened. She required assistance to ride. Jenna sat in front of Kate who controlled the reigns.

Kate worried, "If she did not get Jenna to Erenhil in time, then she would be lost to them forever.

After a pace-stay of weary travel, the two women collapsed with exhaustion. They successfully reached Emmerdale, a small trading hermit on the further reaches of Erenhil borders.

Gareth Nightcrawler disguised as a Kali tradesman, was a sentinel of Erenhil. He recognized the women as Kate and Jenna entered gate.

He greeted them. "Hiyo ladies, what bring you so far from home?"

"Our business is our own. Thank-you very much," replied Kate sharply.

"I mean yea no offence."

"I am sorry. My friend," indicated Kate "is unwell. We have need of shelter and some rest."

"Aye, I have eyes to see with, 'Tis clear to see," he stated, as he caught Jenna as she was trying to dismount from atop of her horse. "Easy, young lady," he stated, as he gently helped Jenna to the ground.

"Ah, thank you."

"My pleasure, Jaknam is my name. Most folk in these parts, call me 'Jake'. If lodging is required, then look no further. I have a spare room. It isn't much. You will find it secluded, private, and free of prying neighbors if you catch my meaning."

"That is very kind, your hospitality is appreciated. Our services are required elsewhere and we shall not be staying long. In-fact, time is running out," interjected Kate.

"Come then, stay as long as you need. I am not too far from here," stated Jake as he guided them to the further edges of the hermitage. After a little while, they arrived at a small hut. "You two go on ahead and make yourself at home. I will tend to the horses. I shall join you shortly."

Kate led Jenna into the hut and when they entered, and laid Jenna on the cot at the furthest end of the room. To Kate, it appeared that Jenna was getting worst. She needed to get some help soon, or Jenna would die. She left Jenna and began to search the room for some kind of medicine that would slow the rate of degeneration that affected Jenna. After a frustrated search, Kate was unable to find anything useful.

A little while later, Jaknam entered the hut. He heard Jenna moaning and went to her side. He pressed his hand on her forehead. Her temperature had risen greatly since he last felt her and he realized that things had gotten worst.

"What is the matter with her," he enquired?

"I do not know. It is some form of magic. Whatever it is, it is affecting her badly and the few medicines I possess offer no relief. If we do not get her to Erenhil, then I fear we will lose her, and with her death, I fear for Lendaw's future."

"Then we have no time to waste," replied Jaknam, he went over to the bed and gently picked her up in her arms, "I need you to press the mantle over by the window."

Puzzled. Kate obeyed and she went to the mantle and pressed the knob, and a doorway opened.

Kate smiled and thought, "I should have guessed," a di-pad portal.

Jenna grew quite faint. Jaknam held on to Jenna, "It is okay Jenna. We are almost there."

"Kate you will need to stand beside me here on this circular disc," continued Jaknam, "Yes, I know who you are. We have been expecting you."

Kate had only used a di-pad portal once and she never attempted it without Alistair present. He explained the theory. It was a magic similar to that of the portal, which brought her to Lendaw. The two pads were interlinked. One only had to stand in the center of the platform and then think of your destination. Jaknam ordered Kate to reach into his vest pocket and remove the crystal key.

"You know how to use it, don't you," asked Jaknam?

"I have used it with the aid of a guide," she replied.

She clutched the key in her hand, turned to Jaknam and said, "Okay Jenna, I need you to think of opening a lock with this key and state Erenhil as your destination." she did what Kate asked, and almost instantly, they all felt a sensation of falling, and indeed they were falling, both, literally and figuratively.

The sentinel guarding the portal turned at the sound in the room. He rushed to the trio. The youngest person appeared gravely ill and to be of near death. She was weak, ashed colored and very cold. "Death would not be too far off," he thought.

"Quick, go get some help," ordered Kate.

"No time for that, we must get her to a healer. Quickly, come with me and please try to keep up," replied Jaknam.

The trio raced through the corridors. It took several arcs to locate a healer. By then, the trio had drawn the attention of most those in the corridors. Word soon spread that a young woman was gravely ill.

Jaknam rest Jenna on a cot.

While Jenna napped, Jaknam explained to Kate who he was. He told her that her pin on her coat alerted him to who they were. He explained that word went out from Erenhil that the guards were to be on alert of a woman and a young travelling companion. He explained that he met her once at the castle and he remembered the brooch. He continued, "Once I knew who you were, I reasoned the young companion was Jenna of whom I heard something about."

It was several pace-stays before Jenna re-awoke. "Well my dear, you gave us quite a fright. How are you feeling?" Jenna tried to sit up. Maia restricted her movement, "You must rest some more."

Jenna felt something around her neck and clasped at the necklace. "It is for your protection. It is the strongest defense against all magical forces that we possess. It is the 'Ara Stia', or 'Blue Star', history tells us it fell from the heavens. It is another gift from the Pantheon. It will protect you from whatever spell that is affecting you. Right now, you need to rest. We will talk more when you are well."

CHAPTER 18

Skirmishes

The Alyran army marched for five-quinti. When it reached Kinell, the troops settled down for some much-needed sleep. The Alyran forces awoke at the sound of alarm. They were under attack by a legion of orks.

The sound of the alarm and the commotion of the troops roused Captain Gareth from his sleep. He quickly clamored out of his tent. He spied the approaching cavalryman and he swerved leftward to avoid his lance. Captain Gareth swung his long sword at the neck of his opponent who fell from the horse with a deadly thud. He gripped the wound in his left arm.

Not too serious.

He was not about to let a slight wound prevent him from entering the battle.

He noted many men and women, partially clad in armor, laid dead or dying at the doorway their tents. Many of them had no chance of defending themselves and they had not even drawn their weapons.

The foe knew exactly when and where to hurt us.

The orks were relentless in their attack.

The battle raged on for over half a pace-stay.

The Alyrans fought one-on-one with the enemy. Each side alternated in taking the lead.

Finally, the Alyrans took the upper hand. The fought back against the last surviving orks who soon retreated from whence they came.

Gareth so desperately wished to pursue them. His orders prevented such action. They were to remain at Ganoll until the rest of ally troops arrived. He ordered some archers to pursuit the fleeting orks. He instructed them to return by days end.

Captain Gareth ordered a count to the wounded and dead. After several arcs, a report was submitted that the number of casualties were not as dire as first believed.

We were lucky. It could have been a lot worst.

"Lieutenant Cartwright!"

"Aye, Captain," he paused as he spotted the gash in the Captain's left arm, "Shall I get some medical aide?"

"It is minor injury. I will attend to it shortly. Send word of our attack to Erenhil immediately and tell them we require their assistance as soon as possible."

"Aye," he replied as he rushed to convey with the messenger.

While the Orkan forces attacked the Alyran forces at Ganoll, Alyra itself came under siege. As the enemy marched toward the castle, hordes of ogres, giants and trolls pillaged the surrounding countryside. Whatever remained behind they torched, or destroyed until nothing useful remained. Luckily, most of the farmers and their families managed to flee to the protection of the castle before the destruction of their lands.

As the enemy turned its attention toward the castle, many occupants inside began to fear. The majority of the Alyran forces were gone to war and the castle had limited defenses. The castle guards and the Lunayr were all that remained to protect the castle and its occupants and neither one, was capable of withstanding an assault of such magnitude.

The onset of the castle started with bombards, medieval cannons, and catapults. The blast and rocks struck the castles outer defenses. The siege of Alyra had begun.

The castle guards defended the castle using longbow archery to kill or maimed as many of enemy as possible. Their attack was futile. They were greatly outnumbered.

Only the Lunayr provided any real defense against the multitude of assailants and their weaponry. The shielding held. For how long it would withstand the onset, no one knew. It was already showing signs of weakness. It crackled with every bombardment.

As the arcs past, the enemy advanced. Outside the main gates, they attached a petard, a small exploding device, they hoped it would blast the gates open and allow them access into the castle. The people and soldiers retreated to the inner chambers and security of the castle. If help did not arrive soon, then Alyra would fall.

As if to answer a prayer, a hail of arrows struck the enemy from behind. The arrows were the first wave of attack. Next in the battle, came the Treent who fought the ogres, giants and Trolls who were no match to their great size and number. The enemy suffered many casualties to their new opponents.

When the Alyrans witnessed the new onset of attack, they rejoined the fight with a renewed sense of hope. They fought with a new vigor and vitality.

The enemy found itself in a battle on all fronts.

After many arcs, the battle ended and dusk appeared over the hills. The Silvan and the Alyran successfully defeated Anko's forces.

"Who is in charge here," asked Caidor?

"I guess, as highest ranking officer, I am. Our captain and our lieutenant died in battle," replied Sergeant Beatle.

"Before we Silvan depart, we will need to discuss the defense of the castle. I will not leave it so defenseless. First, send word to Erenhil of the events here. When you have completed that errand, meet me in the courtyard and we will discuss plans for the safety of Pandora."

About a quintus after Jenna and Kate used the di-pad portal, Donar and the other Shadeen destroyed Emmerdale.

The village of Emmerdale was a peaceful trading post. The proximity to Erenhil and its central location between Pandora and the Free Lands made it an ideal rest point for many weary travelers. Dwarves, free folk, elves, and all the other races passed through its gates. Riders and drifters came to, and fro, throughout the day to trade their wears, treasures, and knowledge. The former was greatly prized. Emmerdale was the hub of information. It was not too large or too small, as to draw attention to oneself. It was the perfect location to discuss intimate subjects. The Shadeen believed Emmerdale to be nothing more than an elven refuge used to gather intelligence of neighboring districts. They sought to destroy Emmerdale and its emissaries. Upon their arrival, the Shadeen discovered it vacant. Its occupants fled to the nearby countryside or to the protection of Erenhil. They missed their opportunity to ambush the trading post. Outraged, they levelled the village and left it in ruins.

CHAPTER 19

Reckonings

Jenna slept restlessly. She tossed and turned, and mumbled incoherently. Days and nights turned to weeks. She awoke to discover Taana by her bedside. Taana continued to nurse her back to health.

Jenna slowly regained her strength. Taana prodded Jenna to eat, and once strong enough, to walk about the chambers or sit out on the balcony. After two quinti, Jenna felt like new. She stretched and yawned and she got out of bed. She briefly washed. She looked in the mirror and she reflected.

I guess the rest had done me good.

Taana entered the chamber.

"Hello Taana. How are you?"

"It is I who should ask you. Well, how are you feeling?"

"I am feeling much better."

"We were worried about you. Let me get you something to wear."

Taana fetched some clothes.

Jenna walked to the table and she took a piece of fruit she found in the bowl on the table. She ate it gingerly.

Taana returned with an outfit. Jenna got dressed while the two women made small talk. A little later Jenna went to explore her new surroundings. She discovered that she felt better than she had in weeks.

The castle she found herself in was made of crystal with hues of blue and green. The immensity of the place was what astonished Jenna the most. The walls were at least ten stories in height, and shined like glass. Except for the room she was in, Jenna found the corridors sparsely decorated. Jenna was in awe. She suspected that all the other corridors within the castle were likewise devoid of furnishings.

There were guards assigned at intervals along the corridors. They greeted her politely with a slight bow as she passed through the hallways. They let her travel freely throughout the castle.

As Jenna turned the corner, she spied Alistair ahead. Before she could call him, he turned and he walked towards her.

"I am glad to see you are well enough to be up and about. You gave us quite a fright. First off, I must apologize for my lapse of judgment. My error caused you great harm, and for that, I am truly sorry. I am afraid that from here on out your movements will be greatly restricted."

"I have travelled these corridors freely. No one attempted to prevent me."

"Or so it seems. There are rarely this many guards throughout the hallways. It seems that you may travel the corridors as you wish just not unescorted."

"We cannot risk abduction. My fault, I know. This is the consequence of that mistake."

"I don't think I can live under these circumstances. I will not be restricted so, and you more than any other, know how stubborn I can when it comes to these issues."

"Then we will have to come to a compromise. We can discuss this matter later. Maia wishes for your company. It is one of the reasons that I sought you out."

Jenna was glad of Alistair's guidance for she would never have found her way to the throne room without his assistance.

Alistair led Jenna to the chamber. As Jenna walked down the aisle toward the throne, the people bowed lightly in greeting as she passed them.

Maia turned her attention to Jenna, "Come and sit here beside me."

Jenna felt unworthy. She did not fully comprehend her new position and she thought she never would. The Queen beckoned her again. Not one to make a scene, Jenna obeyed and sat beside Queen Maia.

"Now that all are present, we shall begin."

Once seated, Jenna took a moment to observe the room. There were many people in the room unknown to her. The few whom she recognized were Kate, Jake, Alistair, and two others whom could only be Danyll and Cryall parents. As she watched them, Jenna felt saddened, and she avoided further eye contact with them.

The meeting discussed the oncoming war, which now seemed inevitable. We received word that Anko's forces invaded Alyra, Kindell, and the trading post of Emmerdale. There is no further doubt Anko is moving against the forces of the light to gain control over all of Lendaw.

Jenna learnt that Anko's forces attacked Alyran forces at Alyra and Kinell. They attempted to attack Erenhil without success, and when this failed, they opted to destroy Emmerdale and its surrounding area in its stead.

Jenna, upset by what she heard, interrupted the meeting, "When did all this occur?"

"It occurred while you were ill."

Somewhat shocked by the news Jenna exclaimed, "I just came through Emmerdale last night."

"You are mistaken Jenna, you have been asleep sporadically for over two quinti."

Confused, Jenna paused to think a second, "if Anko forces are on the move, then there is news I need to share with you. It might be significant."

Jenna took another moment to determine where to begin, "While I was Anko's prisoner, he tried to recruit me as his apprentice. During this time, I discovered something that I am sure I was not meant to see."

Upsetting as it was, Jenna reiterated the events of the last few weeks. She explained about the practice of Vis Colli: the bloodstone and Ka, the source from which Anko derived his power.

Jenna continued, "He acquired the Iluminar from me and without I was powerless."

Jenna broke down. The angst and pain, of the last few weeks, caught up with her and for the first time in quite a while, she cried.

"I believe a recess is in order," stated Maia, as it became apparent to all that Jenna was not ready to face the rigors of everyday life at this time.

"I told you Alistair that she still unwell," Maia stated simply. The trio departed the throne room and went to the royal chambers. They settled Jenna down on the settee and provided food and drink. "We should have discussed the past six quinti in the privacy of my quarters."

When Jenna calmed down, she stated, "I made an ass of myself in there."

"Nonsense, you simply took on responsibility much too soon. After the ordeal you went through, anyone in your situation would have done the same. Think no more of it. You will rest further, and we will talk some more later. Alistair and I have more business to attend. Try not you worry," Maia gently prodded Jenna back on the settee. "I am fine you don't need to baby me. Honestly, I am better. I am coming with you. I am adult and I demand you treat me as such," protested Jenna, as she got up, "are you coming?"

As they returned to the throne room, Jenna reiterated the events of the past few weeks. Alistair listened intently while Jenna discussed Vis Colli, Ka, the bloodstone, and his desire to recruit Jenna. He always suspected that Anko practiced the dark art of his late master Urian, the first Overlord of Ugland, who died during the first Great War. Many people believed that Anko played a part in his demise. As he digested this new information, an idea formed in his mind.

As the trio entered the chamber, Jenna was surprised that the meeting was still in progress. When the party first entered the room, the generals and other officers who were reading over maps and discussing military strategy stopped. After permission by Maia, they continued with their plans.

Jenna sat on Maia's right, while Alistair sat on her left. The two whispered back and forth. Listening in was impossible because Jenna did not understand the dialect they were speaking.

Maia beckoned the meeting to order.

"General Adilyah will you please brief us on current events?"

"You Highness, our informants tell us that there are no Ugland forces in Alyra or Kindell and that they have fled to the fields of Kregen near Mount Kalla. It appears that this is where the enemy will make its stand. We have reached a consensus that we will continue to meet the Alyrans at Ganoll and from there we will continue our march to Kregen. WE believe the attacks by the enemy were a test to determine our resolve and our taste for battle. In this, they were greatly mistaken. Already, the Loren travel, with all haste, to Ganoll to join our Alyran brethren."

"Then, it has begun, thank-you General. When do you think our forces will be ready to depart?"

"We require only another pace-stay to finalize our departure. We should be in Kindell in two quinti."

"Very well, finalize the arrangements and depart as soon as possible. Time is of the essence."

The General bowed, turned, and departed with many of the forces present.

"What of you Alistair? Have you decided?"

"I believe so, your Highness. I can see no other option."

"Very well, I will send a troop of my finest warriors with you. You shall protect her at all cost. Is that understood?"

"I understand and with my life I promise she will not be harmed."

Jenna realized that Alistair and Maia omitted her from discussions yet again!

"What is this? What is happening?"

"It is just an idea. There is nothing definitive. First, I must know. How are your powers? Can you use your powers yet? Have you tested them?"

"I haven't, no? Why?"

"Before I can answer, we need to test your powers. This is not the appropriate place. There is something I need to show you," replied Alistair smirking, "I should have shown it to you when you became my apprentice. There is no time like the present. Will you come with me?"

CHAPTER 20

Unexpected

"Drip, drip, drip," the sound was intense and it gave her a headache.

What, where am I?

The ground she laid on was hard and cold. It was smooth as a well-formed crystalline glass. This was unlike any cavern she had seen before. The underground biosphere was unlike anything they ever witnessed before. The light emulated above looked artificial to her. Its source was strange and unknown. She gazed about her environment before she spied him.

Gently she nudged him. She whispered, "Wake up. Come on, get up."

He stirred, and then he sat up. He shook his head to clear it. His vision was blurry and he had difficulty focusing. His head felt like it was going to explode. "What happened? Where are we? How did we get here?"

All good questions, she knew. The answers were shortcoming.

Finally, she replied, "I do not know. The last thing I remember was falling."

"Me too," answered the male.

The two decided to explore their new surroundings. They quickly discovered that the adjoining chambers were unlike the first. They were earthen. The dirt grew strange vegetation with pockets of crystalline stalagmites scattered about.

"Where do you think this is?"

"I do not know. If I had to hazard a guess, then I would say an artificial sphere of unknown origin. I have never seen such a thing before."

Wherever they were. It was evident that they have been here for some time. The male had grown a beard and they both had longer hair.

"How could such a place exist?"

The two companions have never seen anything like it. They explored the inner hollows layer by layer. Whatever this place was, it was massive. Leaves of green and gold lined the cavern walls like ivory on the castle outer walls and covered the ground like grass in the fields. The vegetation seemed to be the only signs of life.

The thunderous roar ahead drew the duo ever forward. They weaved through the cavern and fissures. They entered a massive cavern and further along they reached the water's edge, the sound was deafening and the mist sprayed them. They scaled downward toward the bottom and the calm stream below.

The male crouched down and cupped his hands. He scooped the water in the palms of hands, he raised his hand to his mouth, and he gingerly drank its contents. The female followed suit. Once they satisfied their thirst, their stomachs immediately began to rumble. They looked around their surroundings. Unrecognizable plants thrived along the riverbank. They dared not risk the chance of being poisoned. The sought another venue. She spotted the fish within the streams of the mighty river. The fastened a net from twigs and vine and they casted their net into the river. Time moved on-ward. They fished until the snagged two fish.

The heard the voice before they spotted its orator.

You require fire.

They looked up and they saw it perched upon the cliff side of the upper cavern. They stared in awe. They saw something that both of them had only heard in folklore. They no longer believe such a creature existed.

Do you not trust your eyes? My brethren and sisters survived. The world continued while we slept. Eventually, time passed and the peoples forgot us. They believed we died out. We did not. We only bid our time, and with your coming, perhaps our time has come as well.

The magnificent creature began its descent from the cliff side. In fear, the two companions backed slowly away from the river's edge.

There is no need to fear. I will not hurt you. My mate and I prevented your fall.

"How is it that we can hear you?"

I am not speaking. I communicate with my thoughts. I am in your thoughts. It is how my kind communicates.

Once upon the ground, the creature spread its huge wings and lifted its head, and it gave a giant roar.

You will have to forgive me. I needed to stretch. I have been in hibernation, so long that I am stiff. I am not as young as I once was. I feel free. It is good to see the world again, even if it is just Undirjord.

"Undirjord, is this where we are?"

Aye, we are in Undirjord the home of the dragons.

"They say, 'You died off'. After the first Great War, the dragons disappeared. Gone, they said to the Netherland and that you were no more."

Nonsense, we only choose to withdraw to this place. Your people had no need of us, so we departed to Undirjord, the ancient fortress of our fathers. We slept. Until such time, that Lendaw required our services again. We would still be asleep except for the explosion. You are lucky that we reached you before you hit the ground. The abyss may look like an endless, but I can assure you, it is not.

"For which, we are truly grateful."

As well you should be, now let us move on to other matters. What of Lendaw, who is this Anko, is he not underling to Urian the 'False One', who was defeated in the last Great War?

"'Underling', you say? You mean Overlord?"

He believes himself to be Overlord, ha - what fallacy is this? His master believed himself to be a god and look what became of him. He perished in the Great War.

"Did he really? There are some who say, 'He only sleeps.'"

Nonsense, I witnessed his fall with my own eyes. He died at the hands of House of Weir. Calanon and Baudhiel, parents of young Turwyn, defeated him. No, we need not worry about Urian. We need to worry about Anko. We must deal with him as soon as possible. Before we can, we must return you to your kindred. It is time for the world to know of the dragons return to Lendaw. We leave for Erenhil at nightfall.

Cryall and Cáel were elated. They were returning home.

You may wish to curtail your enthusiasm by now your family and friends may believe you to be dead. You have both been here for many quinti. We placed you in a type of stasis until your wounds healed, or until you died. We were unsure as to the outcome. It was all that we knew to do to keep you alive. I, for one, was pleasantly surprised when you awoke.

The flight of dragons met at the opening of the Weir. Not for many eons had anyone ridden upon a dragon, and after much debate and argument, the Dracon reached a consensus to allow the two elves permission to ride upon two of their kindred; hence, it was that two persons rode upon Dragon-kind. Cáel mounted Kur and Cryall mounted Ena, and Kur began to sing:

>*Night falls, and darkness comes*
>*The ancients take their flight*
>*Soaring high on wings of lore*
>*They ride through the night*
>
>*Ride through the night*
>
>*N'ver before, nor e'er again*
>*Will the world, witness such a sight*
>*As two riders on the gods supreme.*
>*All others take delight.*

The elves of Erenhil looked up the predawn sky. What they beheld filled them with awe. Dragons, it was beyond all hope. The dragons lived. Their sheer number and their beauty filled them with delight. The dragons circled the city. At last, two broke from their flight and they started to descend. The male was larger and wore a green coat, while the female was blue and a slightly smaller each extended their large legs and spread their wings to slow their decent and as they prepared to land.

The joy that the multitude experienced paled in comparison to their initial delight when they realized who the seated passengers were upon the backs of the pair of dragons.

Maia, Alistair, and Jenna exited the castle as the pair of dragons made their final landing maneuver. Jenna was shocked to see Cáel and Cryall atop the pair. She struggled with her emotions as to whether to laugh with glee, or cry in gratitude. Before anyone could stop her, she bolted for Cáel who was still perched upon the male.

Hiyo, young mistress, forgive me my Lady, I did not recognize you at first. The lad will be down in a bit and then you can become reacquainted.

"I hear you. How is it that I can hear you and that you hear me without speaking," thought Jenna?

Jenna hesitated. After Cáel managed to dismount safely from the male, Jenna rushed to him, hugged, and kissed him. She started to cry. She was never so happy to see anyone in her life. Their lips parted and the two lovers separated. Jenna stood facing him and then she suddenly slapped him across the face. "Don't you ever leave me," she shrieked, "Do you hear me? Never leave me like that again. I don't think I could live through that again."

She hugged, kissed him again, and then cried some more. When she finally calmed herself, she remembered her place. She turned to face the others in their company. Embarrassed she made her apology and offered a full fledge smile, all the while holding hands with Cáel.

Alistair approached Cáel, gave him a hug, and stated, "I am only sorry your father could not be here. I doubt he even knew you were gone. He has been away. We shall meet up with him in the next quintus or so. We are to rendezvous with him, the Loren and the Alyran forces in Ganoll."

While Alistair greeted Cáel, Cryall went and greeted her parents.

All were elated that the two companions returned.

When all the commotion ebbed, the crowd turned their attention to the two great beasts.

> *To Lendaw's plight*
> *The vow promised long ago.*
> *We dragons fight*
> *Against the foe.*
> *Come life, or death*
> *It matters not.*
> *We respond to the threat*
> *To cleanse this rot.*

Hiyo, long have we been absent from the world, no more, no longer shall we lay in hiding while the world cries out for assistance. You respond, and so shall the dragons.

Queen Maia approached and bowed, "You honor us."

Non-sense, we are all in this together. The Hatchlings have explained what has little they could.

"Then you may meld with me," replied Maia, "I may have the answers you seek. I am leader. As such, I am the best person to merge with."

To get a better understand the history of Lendaw since the time of the Great War, Kur scanned Maia's mind. From it, he discerned all the information that he required. When he completed his reading, he apologized for the intrusion and he thanked her for the information. He, and through him, his people acquired the history of Lendaw. They now had a greater understanding of the current events threatening Lendaw.

Kur and Ena turned their attention to Jenna. They lowered their heads and gave a slight refrain that the others seemed not to hear:

> *Calanon, Baudhiel al Turwyn – Three*
> *Blood of my blood*
> *Our daughter be*
> *Joined and united*
> *Our family tree*
> *Sacrifice made*
> *We live because of thee.*

"I don't understand," thought Jenna.

Our families are one. During the Great War, a plague nearly obliterated my people. By chance, your family saved us. We are indebted to you and your descendants. During the Great battle, the accidental mingling of our bloods provided my kind with a cure of the disease that nearly destroyed my people. Your blood runs in us and our blood runs in you. Our two clans then became one. The name: 'Weir' is not just your last name. It is an identity. It is who you are. You are one of the weir.

Jenna was puzzled. The gathered assembly seemed to be unaware of their brief interaction.

Shush, the others must never know – not ever. You must keep the oath. It is enough to know we are bonded. To speak of it would bring great danger to both of us.

CHAPTER 21

Schemes

Upward they went. She thought Alistair would hole himself with the castle. She erred. Upward they scaled. Jenna and Alistair entered the upper chamber on the far side of the castle. It was circular in shape, which made sense since this was in the castle's southeast tower. Alistair explained that he preferred the southeastern view. It provided a picturesque view of the landscape, and more importantly, it permitted him an unobstructed view of Mount Kalla.

Jenna believed herself to be quite a bookworm. She had nothing on Alistair. His collection was immense. The volumes of books and scrolls sat on shelves that surrounded the walls and a pile sat upon the desk in the center of the room.

Jenna sneezed, "Excuse me."

"I am sorry about the mess. I have been absent for many cycles, or months as you call them, and I have not had a chance to tidy up."

To say the room was untidy was an understatement.

Strewn papers, notes and parchments laid about the room. They lay discarded as if someone had left in a hurry. The dust settled on everything, and it was more than a third of an inch thick. The room was damp, and it had a moldy odor. It was quite apparent that no one had been in this room for a very long time.

As if reading her mind Alistair commented, "I have not been in this room for many years. I have been busy searching and wondering through the worlds. Besides, I never had a reason to return here that is until now. Illumino," and the lamps, scattered throughout the room, lit up.

"Now where are they?" Alistair searched the top of his desk and then its drawers. "I know they are here somewhere. Now let me see," he walked over to the bookcase behind the desk and grabbed a black box, and he opened it. "Ah, here they are."

Alistair pulled out two items, handed them to Jenna, and stated, "Should anything happen to me. These will act as proof that I have named you heiress, and that I have left you all of my possessions."

"What are these," asked Jenna?

"The ring of Merlin and my seal," replied Alistair simply. "And I do not want you to argue about it. Everyone knows that you are my apprentice, and that you are the rightful heir. There was another," Alistair paused and mourned the loss, "he chose a different path – one that I could not condone."

Jenna obeyed. She took the two items and she placed them in the pocket of her tunic.

"Now that we have that matter taken care of I must warn you the next phase of our journey will be a perilous one. One, or both, of us may not come out of this alive. Since the fate of Lendaw and of Earth relay upon our success, we must make the attempt. Yes, now that Anko is aware of your world he will not resist conquering Earth. After he has secured Lendaw for himself, he will turn his attention to Terra."

Earth, it seemed so distant now. At the mention of its name, Jenna pined for home. She missed her parents and she wondered how they were doing. A tear ran down her cheek. She wiped it away. She missed the conveniences of her life on Earth: cars, buses, television, the internet and her mobile. None of that mattered any more. She learnt to embrace Lendaw for its simplicity. She loved the freshness of its air, its dazzling beauty, and its people. She wasn't about to stand by and let Anko destroy either world.

Alistair interrupted her thought by saying, "Before we can continue further, we need to ensure that your powers have been restored."

For the next several arcs, Jenna and Alistair practiced their Teleclero. They traded between offensive and defensive positions. When Alistair was convinced that her powers were normal, they stopped to rest. It proved to be a productive day.

"Are you rested? We are required elsewhere."

Jenna nodded, "Yes."

Maia and her court were already in session by the time Alistair and Jenna arrived. The two made their apologies and took their appointed places near the Throne.

"As I explained," stated Aen, the Altmer High Guard, "The enemy forces are heading to Kregen. There are many enemy forces scattered throughout Lendaw. Lucky for us, their number is small and they do not pose a great threat. We easily neutralized them. In so doing, they hamper our progress and they cause us to deplete our much needed supplies."

The war council debated and discussed many different scenarios and strategies to combat them. After more than half a day, Maia rose, and addressed her people, "I believe we have discussed all the possible outcomes and some possible solutions. This is war and all that we can hope for is to plan the best we can and then hope then for the best. Lendaw depends on our success. We cannot let her down. You know your assignments, and you know what is required. I do not order you to your fate. I only ask that you will respond to the need. The hour is now. The need is dire. Who will fight? Who will defend? I say we all, for Lendaw!"

When the chamber emptied of the troops, only Maia, Alistair, Jenna, Cryall, Cáel and a few guards remained within.

"Phase one has begun. Aen will lead our troops to Ganoll. They will mobilize there with the Alyrans and with Captain Hamilton. What of our next plan," enquired Maia?

"I believe that this can only truly end if, and only if, the prophecy is fulfilled. Anko must die. We must break his clutch on Lendaw. Jenna and I must conduct this phase alone. I have a plan. It is risky."

Cryall and Cáel stepped forward and stated, "Not without us." They made their views strongly voiced that the any plan must include them. They would all be included, or none at all. Cáel walked over and took Jenna's hand.

"You might as well include me then," replied Kate, as she entered the chamber. "Charles is dead. I have sensed it for a while. Captain Gareth confirmed it a little while ago. We conversed through the Gaper. A gift I gave him before he left with Charles. Charles died. The army is mainly intact and it approaches Ganoll as we speak."

The group grew solemn at the announcement of Charles death. Charles demise brought home the reality of the dangers involved with what the group attempted to accomplish.

"We are sorry for your loss," stated Maia as she hugged Kate.

Kate shrugged, "It matters not. If fate allows it, I will grieve later. What matters more is that Alistair and Jenna are successful and united we can assure their. I resolve to aide in this quest, or I die in the attempt. I am not of Lendaw, but it is the only home I know."

"Can you get the explosive that I requested," asked Alistair?

"I have the parts. I scavenged from my ship. It will bring the mountain down," replied Kate simply, "though I thought you did not wish to use technology from another world."

"I've changed my mind," stated Alistair simply.

Alistair laid out a plan that would have them enter MarGraven, find and confront Anko and then destroy the mountain, if required. They deliberated on how to best to defeat Anko for the last time. When they had completed their strategies, Maia dismissed them all to their appointed tasks.

Alistair looked at Kate with some trepidation, "Do you see any alternative?" he asked.

Kate shook her head.

"Then you had best get to it. I will see you tomorrow."

Kate turned and left the chamber.

"What was that about," asked Jenna as she and the others approached Alistair?

"It is nothing," he replied.

The others were skeptical.

Jenna sensed that this was a weapon of last resort.

CHAPTER 22

To War

The horse hooves clonked upon the hard rock and the equipment rumbled as they travelled along the road and the noises were a telltale sign of their approach. The noise was unavoidable given the supplied they lugged hauled.

Travel was difficult due to the constant downpour. The blinding and torrential rain made conditions unbearable. They were miserable. Captain Gareth and his men were wearied and disheartened. Their journey to Ganoll was slow and tedious. The men had grown ever more irritable. They fought and argued with each other over the slightest agitation. Morale was at an all-time low. He felt no better.

Just three more pace-stays, until Ganoll, then we can prepare for the coming conflict. I would rather to fight than to continue this humdrum existence. If I die, then it will be for what I have trained for, for most of my life. There are worst things than dying. If the reason is just and pure, then my death will be meaningful and there is no greater cause than the salvation of Lendaw.

The distant thunder Captain Torpek roused from his thoughts. An army approached from the southwest. He held up his arm to signal his men to stop. His scouts arrived to inform him that an army of dwarves approached. It was two arcs before the dwarf army appeared in view.

The army of dwarves marched alongside the Alyran force. The dwarves numbered twenty-five hundred strong.

"Hiyo," hailed Bilpin.

"Hiyo," replied Deskin and Gentwer. The four had not met since they were at Alyra during Jenna's training.

"Deskin and Gentwer, welcome, how goes the day? Where is Sir Hamilton? How are Jenna and the gang?"

"Things are as well as can be expected. Lord Hamilton is dead and there is no word from the others," they replied, "Gareth is captaining now."

The two introduced Captain Gareth to Bilpin and Durkin. They explained to the two dwarves how Lord Hamilton died. Namely, how Lord Hamilton attacked the monster, and how he procured their escape from the Doren Gorge. Captain Gareth interjected and he explained that while they lost some men, the army was almost intact.

"I am sorry to hear this. He was a good man," Bilpin paused, "We too loss many of our people. We are all that remains of my people. My people are near extinction. I am King Bilpin and this is my brother Durkin."

This news shocked Captain Gareth who managed to retain his composure and remained stoic.

"My men are in need of rest. We have travelled far and without much sleep. We must make camp and leave this path before we are discovered," stated Bilpin as he pointed to the vale on the left.

The two companies quickly erected base. While the men and dwarves ate and refreshed their refreshed, the leaders met to discuss strategy.

The journey to Ganoll was near at hand. The risks between here and there were many.

The first night proved uneventful. The scouts departed at dawn and the two companies followed shortly behind. They chose to avoid the trails and roadways, and they opted instead to travel via the hills and vales of the countryside. The hills and vales provided much needed camouflage for the large group. It likewise made their journey slow and hazardous. The party travelled few confrontations. It was nightfall before the senior officers grew concern for the absent scout parties. The scouts failed to report back as ordered. The officers ordered the campground secured.

The combat stared shortly after the troops bedded down for the night. The hostility alerted the sleeping soldiers. Roused from sleep, the men and dwarves scurried to mount a defense.

The shouts went up throughout the camp.

Durkin grabbed his hammer and he leapt through the tent. He struck at the first ork he encountered. The ork dropped to the ground with a thud. Durkin swung the mighty hammer with all is might as the enemy approached. One-by-one each fell to the waste side.

Bilpin stood back-to-back with his brother as he wielded his sword at those who confronted him. He slew them with his sword.

Meanwhile the Alyrans and the Dwarves continued to battle side-by-side. No matter how hard the two allies fought the enemy who continued to advance. The number of orks and gnomes seemed endless and the enemy was ruthless. The foe fought without mercy. The allies doubted that they could maintain the pace. Still the adversary came.

It was, nearly, dawn when the trumpets blared. Captain Gareth and Bilpin glanced to see its source and they were greatly surprise. The elves mounted on horseback raced behind the band of orks and gnomes. Their arrows overwhelmed the enemy who rushed to flee the onset of arrows. By the time that the elves attained the encampment, the opponent was practically defeated. The few foes that remained retreated into the surrounding hills and vales. Captain Caidor ordered his men to pursuit the enemy and he warned them to return by nightfall.

Captain Caidor dismounted his horse and gave it a gentle pat. He marched up to Captain Gareth. Bilpin and Durkin, slightly bowed, and greeted them, "Sal Tel Doe e Paevast, I am Caidor of the Silvan. Am I correct, in assuming, that I am addressing the leaders of this military?"

"Yes, I am Captain Gareth. This is King Bilpin and his brother Durkin."

"We must talk in private. There are things that need to be discussed."

The leaders went on ahead while the troops tended to the injured and dead.

When they were alone, Caidor informed them that their scouts were dead, and that the enemy forces destroyed Emmerdale. The new plan, he informed them, was for the armies to march as quickly as possible to the Fields of Kregen. They were to abolish any, and all, enemy forces they encountered along the way.

"What of Aen and the Altmer," enquired Bilpin?

"They are delayed. I am unsure why. If I had to guess, then perhaps the enemy delayed their arrival."

Caidor explained that the nemesis had numerous scouting parties, troops, raiding parties, and spies scattered throughout Lendaw. He warned them that as one neared Mount Kalla, it was almost impossible to avoid rival contact. Anko's forces now ruled the southern territories.

With the knowledge that the enemy was not far behind, they realized that they destroyed the heavier equipment. The arbalest or giant strong bow, and the catapult had to go. Captain Gareth was disheartened when they destroyed the weapons. He and his men trudged the equipment a long distance. Regrettably, they destroyed them and yet they regretted their actions. It was a shame.

Without the heavier equipment, the army travelled quicker through the forest and lanes. They headed south and travelled a pace-stay before turning east to Kregen. It was a small deter, and one, that they believed the enemy did not expect. They hoped that the mounts and hills alongside the Andar Mountains would provide some cover for the approaching army. To be extra cautious, they marched only at night.

CHAPTER 23

Old Man

Alistair insisted that Jenna, Kate and he travel to MarGraven alone. The others, especially Cryall and Cáel, insisted that they join the quest. They argued that it was folly on their part to go it alone. They reasoned that there were too many unknowns. Even if most of the enemy forces were off to war, it was reasonable to assume that Anko was well guard. After much debate, they simply stated that either they all went, or none at all.

Thus, it was that Jenna, Alistair, Kate, Cryall, Cáel, and two guards departed the safety of Erenhil.

Kate took the lead. She guided the band of followers. As they journeyed toward Mount Kalla, Kate was careful to keep the rucksack that she carried close to her. She permitted no one else to handle the package.

The plan was a simple. Seek out and destroy Anko and all who dared get in their way. The killing Anko was their ultimate goal. They realized it was no easy task with a handful of people against an unknown sized army. The task seemed impossible, yet there was no way around it. Alistair and Jenna were the only two who stood a real chance at defeating Anko. They knew it and so did their colleagues.

Disguised as a guard, Kate led the party through the entrance of Mount Kalla. Their travels were going well until they descent down the lower chambers. Suddenly, guards in the corridor attacked them. The sentries unsheathed their swords and began to fight. Kate and Cáel joined their ranks while Cryall led Alistair and Jenna ahead.

It was not long before they found themselves ambushed by guards protecting the passageways. The trio battled the four guards blocking their passage. They fought side-by-side until the guards laid unconscious on the ground.

Cryall, Alistair and Jenna continued down the passageways. Further and further, the trio descended.

Cryall halted. She indicated with her hands that she had heard a noise. She told them to wait while she went on ahead to investigate. Shortly afterward, the Alistair and Jenna heard a commotion and then fighting. By the time they came to Cryall defense, they discovered they were too late. Cryall sat gasping for breath. She clutched her side with the palm of her hand to prevent further blood loss. Alistair bent to attend to her wound.

"No time for this. You must continue without me. The others will be by shortly. Quickly, time is of the essence," wheezed Cryall. "I will be fine. I cannot continue the way I am. Go, go," pleaded Cryall.

Cryall waited until they were out of sight. She managed to remain alert. She sighed before she passed out.

Jenna and Alistair continued onward. Weaving through the underground passages, Jenna queried Alistair, "How much further until we reach Anko's lair?"

"Not much longer, Jenna we are almost at the Chasm of Rake. From there, it is just a left, then right, right again, further on and then a left until we reach the throne room. Let us make haste. Stay alert."

They travelled the corridors as quietly as humanly possible. So far, their luck was holding out. This soon changed.

"What is that? I heard something."

"Hold back while I explore ahead."

Alistair progressed forward.

Jenna lost sight of him.

It was not long before a scuffle occurred. The sound of staffs clashing, the surge of magic rebounded through the corridors, the cavern shook with explosions, and thunder filled the air. The sounds of men doing battle continued. Kael cried out in pain, and he fell to the ground.

Alistair gave a quick thought.

One down and two to go, though the fight was far from finished.

Enraged, Donar and Anko charged at Alistair who avoided their onset by leaning leftward. Alistair raised his staff and struck them both with a powerful surge that Donar easily countered.

The combat raged on for several more moments with each striking blows and then deflecting them. Back and forth, they battled.

Alistair began to tire. Somehow, he summoned the strength to continue the fight. He fought against his two opponents with all his might.

Donar wield such a blow that Alistair's staff cracked in half. When the staff broke, it let off a tremendous blast. Alistair fell and collapsed to the floor.

The force of the explosion caused parts of the ceiling to fall. In the process, Donar and Anko were injured. Afraid that the cavern would collapse, the two opponents escaped while Alistair lay dying.

Jenna heard the battle and commotion up ahead. Without thought for her safety, she charged forward. When she arrived, she found she was too late.

This is becoming a habit.

"Jenna, what are you doing here? I asked you to stay."

"I waited for what seemed like forever, and then I heard fighting and shouting. I followed the directions you gave earlier. I am glad I came. Are you all right? Oh God, you are hurt. Can you move? Who is that laid out upon the ground?"

"Do not panic. Anko and two of the Shadeen ambushed me. I managed to fight them off. I slayed Kael, and then I focused my attention to Anko and Donar. During the battle, Donar broke my staff and it exploded. The resulting explosion shook the cavern and caused the stalactite and some struck Anko and Donar. They are injured. They escaped. I, on the other hand, am not doing as well. I am dying. I cannot move. There is too much blood loss. I cannot stop it."

"You can't die! I need you. I cannot do this on my own. I don't know what to do. You think I am the appointed one. I am not. I am just Jenna – a girl from another world – not some mighty warrior you made me out to be. I cannot do this alone. I have no idea what to do."

"Jenna, don't cry. Everyone dies. I have to tell you something and this is very important. Anko had a piece of the Gentra with him. I believe he is using it to intensify his power. For a long while, I searched for an answer.

I should have reasoned it out sooner. How could I have been so stupid? The answer was right in front of me. It was obvious. I thought the crystal destroyed. I should have realized that some fragments remained, and that they still held useable power. I was foolish. I must be getting old."

Alistair handed Jenna a pendant. It was the Iluminar.

"How did you?"

"I snatched it from him during our battle. I was once quite the thief in my youth," Alistair chuckled, "After all these years, I have not lost my touch. I don't think he knows it is missing as yet."

Jenna placed it around her neck and she tucked in under her shirt.

"Listen to me. You have the Iluminar. The Pantheon gave it to your ancestors in order to counter the power of the Gentra. You now have the means to end this. Remember your training. Trust in the magic. Believe in yourself."

Alistair gasped for a breath, "One more thing, you are something different. You are more than you know. There has never been a mixture of Druic and Terran before. Never, you are special. When I first spotted you, I knew that I had found what I was searching for, you are spec…," Alistair gasped a breath, slowly exhale, and he was dead.

Jenna desperately shook Alistair and screamed, "Alistair, don't die."

Jenna sobbed and sobbed until it was painfully obvious that Alistair was gone. Jenna rocked Alistair in her arms. She cried and cried, until the tears subsided and she could cry no longer. She was alone. Her teacher, and mentor, was dead.

She kissed Alistair on the forehead, and she laid him gently on the ground.

It was then that she noticed his blood on her hands. She wiped the blood against her pant legs. After she stroked the last remaining tear from her eyes, Jenna rose to her feet.

She felt terrible abandoning Alistair. She had no other alternative. She had to continue without him. People depended upon her. She struggled to move forward and she took her first step into the unknown.

CHAPTER 24

Battle of Kregen

Hence, the armies of the world met on the Fields of Kregen. The forces of the light and the forces of the dark stood opposite each other ready to battle.

The Anko's forces lined up. The giants and the orks took the front position. Their appearance was like an impenetrable wall sheltering the infantry. Some of the Alyrans grew anxious.

Durkin was strangely unmoved. He gripped the mighty axe tightly, with is right hand, and he immediately sensed its power. He was sure that giants and orks stood very little chance of withstanding the power of the Mjolnir. He believed that he could break through the enemy front line and create a pathway for attack.

"Durkin what is happening," asked Bilpin?

"We are waiting for the hammer to fall," he sneered. "The incessant waiting is starting on my nerves. I wish the battle would start, so we can be done with it."

"You will get your chance. Be careful what you wish for, you just might get it. War is no laughing matter. It is messy business, and it is not to be made light of."

"I know, I know. I am tired of waiting we have been waiting for three pace-stays now. What became of Jenna and Alistair? Is there any word of them?"

"The last I heard was that they went on to MarGraven unescorted. I fear for their safety."

"You're worried for their safety, what about ours? Do you give no thought of our own? Can you not see that we are out-numbered ten to one?"

"Brother, I see well enough thank-you. I just have to hope that is all. I do not know about you, I am counting on Jenna and Alistair to finish all of this. I do not care how they accomplish it. I only care that they finish it."

"If she does and I hope you are right, then may Griminar be praise!"

Captain Gareth took this time to address his men, "We who are about to fight this day. We do, so for all we hold dear: For Queen and country, yes. We fight to protect all that we love of Lendaw. We fight against the plague that would affect the land. We fight to keep Lendaw free. It is our charge. It is our duty. Who will rise up to protect our lands, our families and all who wish to free of tyranny? Let us take up the sword and our weapons. Who will fight, who will join me in this great struggle? Let us fight and never surrender until we send the enemy back to the abyss from whence it came."

The Alyrans stood ready. They grasped their weapons and prepared to attack.

"Look, something is happening at the front! It looks like you will get your wish. Griminar be with us," shouted Bilpin.

The battle commenced with the onset of longbow arrows. The arrows pierced those in the first few rows of the army of light. The Alyran allies return the volley, and some of the front-line Uglandan forces fell. The barrage continued. Both men and beasts fell in their wake.

Suddenly, the enemy then raced forward.

Durkin never hesitated. Upon seeing the enemy charging, he rushed bravely forward to meet the challenge. Durkin met the enemy head on. He swung the axe directly at the foe.

Bilpin, upon witnessing this, feared for his brother. The axed changed him. Durkin acted as one possessed. He raged onward through the enemy front lines without a single thought for his own safety.

The first giant tumbled leftward and smashed into his companions knocking the three of them over. He swung to the right with similar results. Just as he suspected with the axe, he was able to punch a hole into enemy lines. Durkin continued swing his axe left and right. The enemy soldiers were no match for the power of the Mjolnir. It did have its limits, which Durkin soon experienced. As with all magic, the Mjolnir had its price. Durkin was quickly tiring, and the axe became too heavy to wield. Durkin stumbled.

Bilpin and the Alyran armies rushed to his aid.

Captain Gareth and his equestrians charged to attack the enemy forces. Fighting from horseback was a difficult and tricky business. The horses proved able to push back the enemy forces. This changed over time. The smell of blood caused many of the animals to panic. Some of the horses died, while others maimed. Eventually, the remaining horses began to retreat. Captain Gareth dismounted his horse 'Lightning', so it could flee to safety. He continued to fight. His example encouraged his men to stand and fight. Meanwhile, the pole-armed troops surrounded Durkin while the Alyran infantry continued the battle threw enemy forces. They fought with all their might. Slowly they pushed ever forward.

While the Alyran and Dwarven armies battled through the central line, Caidor and the Silvan troops divided in two with each taking the left and right flanks. They fought the enemy with arrows and in hand-to-hand combat. Caidor's initial trepidation about dividing his troops was unfounded. The Silvan fought with all their might. Despite Caidor's initial worries, the Silvan succeeded in causing the enemy to fall back.

The battle raged on for more than half a pace-stay, the forces of the light managed to hold our own. They fought long and hard. They did not know for how much longer they would hold their ground. No one could say. Even with the power of the Mjolnir, they took on heavy causalities about a third of their forces were either dead, or too injured to fight. The number of dead made fighting difficult. Blood filled the field, making it slippery, and thus, more dangerous to fight.

The men fought onward. Hopelessly out numbered, they needed re-enforcement, or they would surely lose the battle. The enemy forces pushed forward. Their numbers knew no bounds. The dwarves and men fought side-by-side.

"I thought the Altmer would be here by now," exclaimed Durkin.

"I thought so too," responded Bilpin, "We could use their help."

The two dwarves fought side-by-side with each protecting the others back.

"Gurr, Bilpin watch your stance and keep up your guard," yelled Durkin as he struck the approaching enemy with his axe, "Are you trying to get yourself killed? I do not wish to see you die this day – keep close and strike true."

"I could say the same to you. I saved your hide more than once," retorted Bilpin.

The Alyrans troops were committed. The battle was in full motion. They could not retreat, lest it meant their demise. They were in a terrible predicament. Their forces were dwindling by the arc. With so many causalities, the Alyrans were beginning to despair.

Then they heard it.

The galloping horses' hoofs reverberated off the dry earth, and roared like thunder across the sky. A happier sight, the Alyrans ever witnessed. As far as they eye can see, elves and men lined the roadway.

Upon hearing the approaching forces, the Uglandan made their retreat. In their haste to escape, the enemy suffered much causality. Eventually, the Alyrans forces let them go.

"Hiyo, Aen how goes?"

"I am sorry, Durkin. We took longer to get here than we had planned. The numerous bands of gnomes and trolls we encountered along the way slowed our progress. Once we realized that their numbers were not too large. We eventually reasoned their ambushes were nothing more than a diversion to slow our arrival. We opted to ignore their attacks and to made haste to join you."

"Your arrival could not have come at a better time. We managed to keep our ground still we have suffered the great loses. We have lost more third of our forces. It seems with your arrival they have retreated."

"I would have to concur. Once the Uglandan forces had taken a break and regrouped, they will return. In the meantime, tend to your wounded and get some rest. My men and I will keep watch."

CHAPTER 25

More Death

When Kate, Cáel and the sentries defeated the corridor guards, they hasten downward through the maze of tunnels until they reached Cryall.

"Good stars," exclaimed Kate, "What happened to you?"

"I was attacked. I am injured. I will live. Alistair and Jenna continued onward. You must go after them."

Kate eyed Cáel and the soldiers who departed immediately. She looked upon Cryall and exclaimed, "You are going to be okay."

Kate reached into her sack, pulled out some Theriac, and handed it to Cryall, "Here drink this."

After drinking the elixir, Cryall felt stronger.

"Now let me tend to your wound. This is going to hurt, so brace yourself."

Kate retrieved a vial and took out an orange cream-like substance. She applied it to the wound at Cryall's side. Upon application, the substance began to bubble and cauterized the wound. Cryall inhaled and held her breathe. The pain was intense, and then later it subsided. Cryall looked at the wound. Except for a dry scab, the substance healed her wound.

"What the Helroh was that?"

"It is Wondhale. It seals and disinfects wounds."

Kate handed the remaining Theriac to Cryall. She explained that this is where they departed.

Cryall was confused. "Are you not coming with us?"

"I have another duty to perform," she replied simply. "We take different paths from here. You must go and protect Jenna."

Cryall got to her feet. She felt better, and she able to function. She looked a Kate. Cryall had a bad feeling. She kept her fears to herself. Instead, she turned to Kate and gave her a warm hug.

"Thank-you for all your help," she paused, "I hope I will see you soon."

Kate nodded, gathered her things, and turned right down a different pathway without any further response.

Cryall was tempted to follow her then she thought better of it. Cryall shrugged her shoulders, she turned, and then she raced downward to catch up with Jenna and the others.

Jenna meanwhile had reached the two fleeing adversaries. She spotted Anko and Donar as they weaved through the labyrinth of tunnels ahead. She casted a spell and she missed her intended targets. Donar, filled with rage, turned to counter-spell while Anko continued to make his escape.

According to Alistair, a Shadeen was difficult to kill. Jenna was unsure she was capable to the task.

A moot point, as Donar would try to kill me either way.

She hoped that she was somehow up to the task. She was about to find out.

The two confronted each other. The battle started with simple spells. With each round, the fight intensified.

It is as if Donar is sizing me up. He is trying to determine my skill and training.

The fighting increased and the spells reverberated off the cavern walls. The corridors trembled and the echo rumbled in response to their assaults.

"You are much stronger than I thought. Alistair has prepared you well still you are no match for me," Donar sneered.

Donar returned the volley. Jenna deflected each blast.

With each success, Jenna grew in confidence and she sensed the tide was turning in her favor. She was winning. Most of her spells struck Donar.

Donar began to panic. He reached into his pocket and he pulled out a piece of the Gentra. The green crystal immediately flared to life and struck at Jenna, who faltered and stumbled backwards.

Jenna struggled to battle Donar. She fell back and she lost her footing. She landed against the cavern wall. Exhausted, Jenna could not summon the power to continue.

I have her now. She is done. I just have to finish her.

Donar casted his final spell. Suddenly, the Iluminar under Jenna's tunic responded and it flared to life. It blocked the power of the Gentra. For this, was the Iluminar created. It responded against the power and might of its counterpart. The spells battled each other and the streams reverberated and echoed. The cavern shook and trembled, and the sound of thunder filled the cavern. Eventually, the spell streams reversed and both crystals exploded in a blinding light.

While the battled commenced, Cáel and the two sentries heard the crashing, and then felt the commotions in the cavern below them. They were unsure as to what to do whether to remain or to leave. Their emotions were tormented either they abandon their deceased friend, or charge to aide another battling below. One companion was dead while another faced great peril. They were perplexed as to what they should do. Cáel made the heart-wrenching decision to continue, he nudged the guards and the trio departed.

Steadily and with great difficulty, they worked their way down through the passages.

By the time Cáel arrived, he discovered both Jenna and Donar unconscious. He went to Jenna and found her breathing. He let out a sigh. Meanwhile, the two guards approached Donar. They discovered that he was dead.

Jenna had somehow managed to kill Donar.

While Cáel was glad that Donar was dead, he worried for Jenna. She was breathing though lightly, and no amount of rousing would wake her. He repeated her name and gently shook her trying to wake her. She remained unconscious.

It was not long before Cryall discovered Alistair lying in a pool of his own blood. She bent down to check for a pulse and bent her head. She sang the Song of Sorrow and shed a small tear.

There has been a lot of death on this quest. She hoped the price was worth it. One friend was dead; another was in a desperate need of assistance.

She arose and she fled quickly down the corridor.

It was half an arc before Cryall appeared.

Cáel gently laid Jenna down. He went to Cryall as tears weld up in his eyes.

"She won't wake up," he repeated.

Cryall slapped him and repeated her question, "What happened here?"

"There was a fight between Donar and Jenna. We stopped to attend Alistair. It was too late. He was already dead. Then we felt the caverns shake and heard the crashing sounds. We decided to desert Alistair. By the time we arrived, we found Jenna and Donar unconscious. Donar is dead and Jenna won't wake up."

Cryall pushed Cáel gently aside. She raced to Jenna's side, knelt down and said, "Let me see what I can do."

She retrieved the vial of Theriac from her pocket.

CHAPTER 26

Standing Ground

The Altmer stood watch as the others ate and relaxed. After a brief rest, some of the Silvan joined them. It had been centuries since the two tribes stood side-by-side. Aen and Caidor discussed the current events before turning the discussion to the history of their people.

At first dusk, a trumpet blared to alert the troops.

The enemy had returned and with them were four Shadeen and their gargon. It appeared that this next phase was going to be more vicious.

Aen turned to Caidor and he stated, "Our people will handle the Shadeen, while the dwarves and men manage the enemy forces."

The Shadeen attacked swiftly, they weave through the army casting their spells while their gargon attacked the tents and animals. The elves countered the spells and they attempted to block the gargon with their magic. It was hopeless. The gargon being part dragon, made their magic useless. They were immune to their spells.

"Caidor cursed. We cannot defeat the gargon. It is pointless to even try." Aen only smiled, he raised his arm, and he released a summoning spell into the night sky.

In answer, a flight of dragons descended from above the clouds. They numbered the gargon six to one.

Kur, Ena and the others were waiting for the signal. They would wait until the two parties were engaged in battle before they made their presence known. They hoped that this action would surprise the Shadeen and prevent their escape. So far, the plan was working.

Kur and Ena engage the lead gargon. The two clawed and bit at the gargon's neck and under belly. The gargon hissed and squirmed as it tried to get away. The Shadeen cursed and pulled out his sword. He tried to defer Kur and Ena's attack. It was futile. Kur attacked while Ena pulled back to safety and vice versa. The Shadeen was no match for the two of them. The other Shadeen were experiencing similar difficulties. There was just no way for them to defeat multiple dragons.

As the battle above raged on, the dwarves and men attacked the opposing army. Again, Durkin found himself in the lead. He swung the Mjolnir at the enemy frontline, which allowed the remaining dwarves and men to attack. The infantry followed on horseback with their riders fighting and widening the opening. They Alyrans and dwarves continued to battle until they pushed back the hoard of attacking orks and gnomes. The archers focus their attention of the giants. The battle was brutal with casualties and deaths mounting on both sides.

The elves continued to fight the four Shadeen who were all busy trying to protect their gargon. Their spells were taking their toll. Already two Shadeen were unsaddled from their beast. They fought with magic and with sword. Caidor struck the first Shadeen who vanished and was gone. When his master died, the gargon fell to the ground, and the beast lay dying. Aen took out the other. There were only two Shadeen remaining.

Kur and Ena battled the gargon until it was weaken. It fell from the sky and hit the ground hard. It landed upon some of them enemy forces killing them instantly. The both went in for the kill. Its rider took out his sword and injured Ena. She managed to stay alift and she fled to Alyran defenses where and she managed to land safely. Meanwhile Kur went in for the kill. It is not easy for one to kill a Shadeen. In his, state of rage, Kur slayed the Shadeen by piercing the heart of the Shadeen with his tail. The Shadeen instantly ceased to exist. Next, he savagely attacked the wounded gargon and he killed it. When he was finished, Kur felt a trill in his kills.

No one injures my mate and lives to tell about it.

The other dragons sensing blood, descended on the last Shadeen and gargon. They fought them until the enemy was no more.

With the Shadeen and the gargon defeated, the enemy forces lost their conviction for battle. They began to waver. The gnomes were the first to scatter.

The giants and orks continued to battle. They both had nothing else to lose. The other races despised them. For ages and ages, the giants and the orks bore the ridicule from the others. They swore their revenge. One day, they would stand above all others in the new order to come. Today was that day. They determined to fight until the end whatever the outcome.

United again, Deskin, Gentwer, and Dwendelmir fought the giants and orks. They battled against the foe with all their might. The trio had not been together since Alyra when they trained Jenna. The fought the enemy without fear and they let no enemy escape. Their valor rallied the others who joined them in the fight. The battle raged on for many arcs and throughout the night. By morn, most of the enemy was dead or fleeing. It had not been an easy battle. They were victorious still there were many casualties. In the mayhem, Gentwer and Dwendelmir experienced minor injuries.

Amazingly to Bilpin's surprise, Deskin escaped unharmed.

CHAPTER 27

An Old Foe

Cryall tended to Jenna as best she could with the limited supplies she carried. After providing some Theriac, and some drink, Cryall had done all that she could do. She could only wait and see. Jenna would have to awake of her own accord.

It was several arcs, before they heard it, Jenna was moaning softly to herself. They did not understand what she was mumbling. They were only glad she was. She was waking up.

After a few more groggy moments, Jenna whispered a question, "What happened?"

"You were unconscious when we found you, so we are unsure. You were fighting Donar."

Jenna tried to get up. Cryall prevented her.

"Do not fret. Donar is dead. You must rest a bit more."

The group sat and ate some snacks. After a while, when it appeared that Jenna had regained her strength, they sat her up. Later, they permitted her to rise until Jenna assured them she was fine.

"I am better. We cannot wait any longer, I still have a job to do, we must continue."

Jenna and her entourage continued through the maze of passages. They backtracked whenever they hit a dead end, which thankfully was not too often. They wondered the cavern going downward and downward.

The company started to get antsy. They knew that their final destination was near and that Anko was within their grasp. They braced themselves against any attack.

Anko met up with Lisstic. He informed Lisstic that the Weir youngling was chasing him. He knew of Lisstic's hatred of the girl. He was willing to use this knowledge to his own advantage.

If Lisstic could deal with the girl, then all the better.

Lisstic hissed, "At last."

Lisstic gathered some men and together they quickly raced up the pathway.

As she turned the next curve, Jenna ducked and then she quickly swerved sideways. She pulled out her short sword and she raised it above her head to block the strike. Her instinct and training kicked in. The battle had commenced. Since she had to react so quickly, Jenna was unaware, with whom she was fighting.

Except for Jenna, Cáel and Cryall found each other fighting two or three foes.

After a few more deflects, Jenna managed to glimpse her attacker. It was Lisstic the reptilian from the Slavidian, who earlier promised to avenge his family for a perceived murder of their Queen at the hand of the Weirs. Jenna knew that she was no match for Lisstic as he was bigger and stronger than she was. She knew she could fight him off for a little while until she tired and grew exhausted. Her only hope was to distract him and to make her escape.

She ducked to avoid yet another of Lisstic's blows.

"At last, I will have my revenge. I am going to kill you girl and I am going to enjoy every moment of it," Lisstic hissed.

The two continued to spare each other, their weapons clashed and clanged against each other. Jenna soon tired. She struggled to continue. Cáel witness Jenna falter, he temporarily managed to dispose of his attackers, and he rushed to her aid. Cáel struck Lisstic's hilt before it could injure Jenna.

"Jenna, go," he pleaded.

She refused to leave. The two of them battled Lisstic who held his ground. As the fighting continued, Cáel previous three opponents got up and they charged forward to attack.

It is now, or never.

Cáel seeing an opening in Lisstic's armor made his move. He thrust his sword upward pass the armor and into the soft underbelly portion of Lisstic's belly. He then twisted the sword sideways and downward. Lisstic dropped to the ground and died.

There was no time to think, his three opponents reached the duo. They fought with Cáel and Jenna until Cáel pleaded with her, "Jenna, you must go. This is not your fight. Go, go." He gently shoved her away from the fight.

Jenna obeyed and she left the scene.

Like Cáel, she knew she was destined for something else.

Grudgingly, she left her companions to their own defenses.

Once again, it seemed the fates forced the couple to go their separate ways.

CHAPTER 28

Destiny

The chamber, which Jenna entered, had a throne on one side, and a dais in the center. The room was the same one she was in previously. The 'whomp' sound filled the chamber. The room reeked of rotten flesh, urine and other waste products. Blotches of dark blood splattered the room.

"Well girl – you've come."

"Anko," Jenna's heartbeat went faster and faster, and her hands began to sweat.

I can't do this not without Alistair.

"He was foolish to drag you into all of this," stated Anko simply, as he waved his arms about.

"He should have left you on Terra where you belonged."

Jenna was terrified of the outcome of this duel. She feared for her life. She began to doubt her abilities and her training, and she wondered if she was capable of defeating Anko. Her mouth became very dry and her hands were sweaty, and she began to tremble.

Why is suddenly so cold in here?

"You should not have come. I do not blame you. No, you are a pawn. You were bought into it by one who believed that you are the fulfillment of prophesy. Yes, I know of it. After our last visit, Donar informed me of what he learnt from Trevik Skay. I know a great many things. I know that Alistair went to Earth to retrieve you in the hopes that you are the chosen one. He was a fool. You are no match for me."

135

He knows. He knows everything.

"I care not whether you are what Alistair claimed you to be. Perhaps you are; perhaps you are not. In either event, I care not. With the power of the Gentra, I am invincible. I defeated your mentor. I will defeat you too. You cannot stop me."

Jenna, you must stay calm. Calm down.

She took a deep breath and repeated. She started to calm down.

I am in this and there is no escape. I have made my choice. I must fight. I can only do my best, or I will die in the attempt. I must not back out-either the prophecy is correct and I am the one, or I am not; only fate can determine which is correct.

Once she decided to fight regardless of the outcome, Jenna felt calm again.

The two opponents circled each other. Each sized the other and each took a guarded stance.

"For many years since I awoke, I searched for the remains of the Gentra. Once I discovered the shard, I learned to yield its power and meld it with my own. With it, my power grew."

Jenna continued to guard herself, "You don't look all that well. Alistair sure gave you quite a fight."

"Don't mock me. I could kill you in an instant," commented Anko as he casted his power.

Witnessing the Gentra come to life, and knowing that she no longer possessed the Iluminar, Jenna prepared to die. The force of the blow knocked her back and she cowered against the wall. She returned the spell though a weak one that caused no harm. Jenna began to doubt.

I cannot do this. I am not the one.

She prepared for death.

The next spell will surely finish me off. I am ready.

When Anko cased his next spell, it struck her. To her amazement, when the force of the spell hit her, it deflected off her. It was then that she began to wander. Was she the Crux? Was she the living embodiment against the power of the Gentra? She was unsure.

The two battled for some moments without a clear winner. Both opponents seemed evenly matched. The struggle continued.

Where have I found myself? This is insane! What was Alistair thinking? What did he say to do, 'believe in the magic and myself'? How could that make a difference?

Jenna faltered ever so slightly and the battle took a turn for the worst. She found herself weakening. Anko sneered and he laughed hysterically.

"The end is nigh, prepare to die."

Weakening still, the power destabilized and she felt the power ebb within her. She feared the worst.

It appeared to Anko that this was the end. Jenna lay on the ground and she appeared to be powerless.

The magic striking Jenna weakened her. She cowered down to her knees and she waited to die.

Then she recalled Alistair's words, "Humans have a strong sense of self preservation and a great will to live."

Jenna remembered all that she had to live for. She recalled Cáel, her new friends, Lendaw, Earth and her parents. She wished to survive. She longed for Earth and pined to reunite with her parents. She yearned to be with them again.

I refused just lie here and let this happen. I will not die. I want to live.

Jenna rose from the ground. She suddenly experienced a renewed strength within herself. Her elven part of her empowered her with magic. Her human side gave her the will to survive. She grew in confidence. She believed in herself and in her abilities. She felt the magic welled inside of her until it seemed she could no longer contain it. The power flared to life. It sprouted ever outward and it grew ever stronger. The intensity of the magic continued to build. As it did, the cavern shook and rumbled until the roof began to shatter. Chunks of rock to fell to the ground. The stream of magic struck the power of the Gentra. The power pressed ever forward. It energy prevailed over the Gentra. Still, the magic thrust forward. It struck the Gentra and it shattered to dust. It was not finished. The magic continued to burn. For the first time since he was a lad, Anko trembled in fear. He realized, too late, that he was mortal. He was about to die. In rage and fury, he let out one more cry before he was gone.

The energy ceased. Jenna relaxed. It was over and somehow she had won. She collapsed.

CHAPTER 29

Completions

"Durkin what's happening? There is a commotion up ahead."

"I am not sure brother. Keep fighting. For your own sake, keep going. I see as well as you the confusion that is occurring. This is no time to stop and wait for orders and watch your side. You almost got it there."

"Don't worry about me. You watch yourself."

"Look, the Uglandan, they are turning and fleeing. Cease fire, cease fire!"

"What is going on? Why?"

"I am unsure. There are rumblings emanating from MarGraven. Perhaps, Jenna succeeded."

Aen step forward and enquired, "What is happening?"

"The enemy appears confused and they are scattering," replied Bilpin.

"Let us pursue them then," replied Aen.

The forces of light continued to attack the opposing forces. The enemy was not retreating to MarGraven instead some they fled southwards, while others ran westward toward the Black Lands from whence they came. They battled the enemy until none remained.

The battle was over. They won.

I did it. I cannot believe it. Anko, Donar, and the rest of the Shadeen are gone. I destroyed all remnants of the Gentra. It is over. It is finally over, though I can't help but wonder. What of the others, are they okay, and do they live?

She shook her head, "No".

I can't worry about them just yet I must get back. Alistair, how my heart breaks, I still can't believe you are gone.

Exhausted, Jenna collapsed.

"Jenna, can you hear us?"

"Here! I am over here."

"What has happened?"

"It is done. Anko is dead. It was all true. I was the answer. I obliterated the Gentra and I eliminated Anko. Maia was right."

Jenna paused and then she resumed, "I am unable to stand. I am okay. I just can't stand. Each time I try to rise; I fall down."

"I will help you," avowed Cáel.

He gently picked her up in his arms. Jenna wrapped her arms around his neck, and Cáel carried her out of MarGraven.

It was some time before they reached the mine adit. When they reached the exit, Jenna insisted Cáel put her down.

Kate freed the captives. She knew what she was about to do and she did not wish to cause others unnecessary misfortune. With the job of setting the prisoners free completed, Kate had just one last duty to perform. She had to place the device deep within the depths of Mount Kalla. She descended the corridors until she reached the furthest pits of the mine.

The plan to bring down the mountain was Alistair's idea. He did not wish others to exploit Mount Kalla for their evil purposes ever again. He witnessed the evil emulating from its depths once too often. He persuaded Kate to bring down the mountain. The fusion bomb she carried would seal the mountain forever and the explosion would contain any harmful radiation within it.

The rumbles, tremors and quakes she felt confirmed to her that Jenna was successful. Alistair explained to her what to expect. She was elated for her. Lendaw was safe. Her friends were safe. She had only to wait for then to make their escape. She waited to bid them time.

The captives of MarGraven made their escape, one such prisoner was Gnoz. Jenna spotted him. At first, she was unsure. She did not recognize him. He was thinner than he once was and he was dirtier too. His eyes were sunken and he appeared listless.

Jenna called to him, "Gnoz, wait."

Gnoz turned at the call of his name. When he saw his companions, he did not believe his eyes. In disbelief, he just stood where he was and he stared.

Jenna called him again while she held out her arms.

They returned for me. They did not forget me.

Gnoz felt cheerful. He rushed to the companions and he flew into Jenna's welcoming arms. They hugged for several moments. For the first time in a long time, Gnoz was elated.

"I am sorry to interrupt this happy reunion. We have got to go," stated Cáel, "get moving and stay alert."

Cáel and his companions drew their weapons. They were dubious of the unknown. They expected to confront the guards or soldiers. They were flabbergasted when they did not. Cáel thought this very odd.

The little party descended the mountainside. They scurried along the paths; downward they escaped to the fields below. By the time they reached the bottom, they were exhausted, scratched and bruised. Jenna did not think she could travel any further. As luck would have it, she did not have to. A party of elves crossed their path. The elves were scrutinizing the field for battle survivors when they happened upon the little assembly. Cryall stepped forward, and she spoke briefly to the Commander whom she recognized. The Commander examined the raggedy troop before him. He ordered his men to offer assistance. The ride back to the encampment was swift.

Kate was sorry that she would no longer see her friends. She was practical about it. She understood. Someone had to do this. She reasoned that it should be her. Charles was gone. Her mate was dead. She knew she could not live without him. She promised Alistair. A vow that she swore she would keep. She was bound to it.

It was Cryall that she would miss the most. When they met earlier, Kate could not bring herself to say farewell. Cryall was the first female to befriended Kate. She taught Kate about life and love. Before then, all Kate knew was duty and death. As a Star fighter of a nasty war, Kate knew only military strategy, training and duty. When Charles first fell in love with Kate, Cryall explained the intimacies of dating and love. These were foreign concepts to Kate. She never knew love. Cryall never laughed or teased Kate over her ignorance in these matters. Instead, Cryall was patient, kind and generous – a true friend.

It is a shame that she could not acquire a detonation device. She had no other option. It needed to be set manually. Oh well, my husband. It will not be long now. I have a promise to keep. We shall meet again.

CHAPTER 30

Aftermath

"So much death," Jenna reflected over the last year.

King Tharin's death and the attempted genocide of the dwarves; Danyll, Lord Hamilton, Alistair, the defeat the Shadeen, the gargon and of Anko. Jenna was, especially, saddened to hear of the loss of Kate Hamilton. A woman whom she had once despised, only to discover a true friend and ally. So much death.

Jenna tried to rest. Sleep proved elusive. Whenever she attempted to lie down, the nightmares followed and she promptly roused from her slumber.

Jenna wondered aimlessly to the burial site. The allies buried their dead with dignity and respect, while they piled and burnt any enemy carcasses they discovered. The disposal of the dead was a necessary chore. Thankfully, she was not involved her with it. It still gave her the creeps.

The result of a pampered life, well that person is gone. The young woman had grown up. She was an adult. She had done and experienced more than she ever thought possible. The shy and timid young woman is no more. Anko was dead, and the Gentra was no more. She successfully completed what they expected of her. Everyone began to treat her with awe and reverence. It made her uncomfortable. She was not any different. At least this was how she felt. She thought herself as no different from anyone. The past no longer mattered. Lendaw was safe.

The few enemy who survived, fled to the hillsides. They ran to seek refuge throughout Ugland and the Bad Lands. They no longer posed any further threat. Those who did pose a threat, the allies dealt with swiftly and harshly. These hostilities were few.

It was the time to bury the dead and to grieve.

The dragons departed that morning. Before they left, they assured Jenna that they would return.

It decision was made, for safety's sake, that the allies would return to Erenhil. From there, each race would depart their separate way to their respective homes. They would leave the fields the next morning.

Jenna wandered freely throughout the camp. No one bothered her and allowed her full access throughout the grounds. She later learnt that Cáel gave orders that if she did not attempt to leave the safety of camp, then she was free to roam the campgrounds. The threat was over. There was no further need to fear for her safety. Besides, she had proven that she was more than capable of taking care of herself.

Jenna went to check on Gnoz. She entered his tent and went to his bedside. He mumbled in his sleep and he slept fitfully. It was obvious to her. He was still not well. No medicine offered to him by the elves proved effective. She approached the healer to discuss his treatment. The two debated as to his next form of treatment. Eventually, Jenna suggested that they attempt to halt his current treatment. She further proposed that they feed him the roots and berries found abundantly around the encampment. She reasoned that as a member of a scavenger race, he probably only ate that which he could procure. She wiped his forehead with a damp cloth and then she departed.

I will check on him again later. I must try to rest.

Jenna returned to her tent. Cáel was asleep on the cot. Jenna crawled into bed and joined him. He mumbled something. He did not wake up. She envied his ability to sleep. Cáel wrapped one arm around her, and after a while, she managed to doze off to sleep."

She woke early in the morning.

Another nightmare, I guess that is to be expected. I probably will not ever again get a good night sleep.

Jenna climbed out of bed. Her movement woke Cáel from his sleep.

He mumbled, "Did you sleep?"

"I slept for a while. I still find it difficult. There are too many nightmares to keep me awake. I am told that this will fade with time."

The two got up and they quickly washed. The water was cold. It felt refreshing. They changed their clothes and left the tent. Later, they took down the tent and packed it away.

Jenna went to check up on Gnoz one final time. When she went into his tent, he was sitting up in bed.

"Are you well enough to travel?"

"I am better."

"You will ride with me and don't bother to argue. We depart in less than an arc and you are still too weak to walk. You must get ready to leave."

"I won't bother to debate the matter. You will not listen anyway. I am ready. All I have are the clothes on my back."

The clothes he wore looked pitiful. They were in an awful state. They looked more like rags than clothes. She would ask Bilpin if the dwarves had something suitable for Gnoz to wear.

"I will go get you some new clothes. When you are ready, come seek me out."

Jenna left and went to Bilpin. He assured her that they would find something suitable for the gnome to wear.

Jenna took one more trip around the base, while the soldiers packed the gear.

The infantry and the equestrians took the lead while the scouts went on ahead to ensure their path was clear.

CHAPTER 31

Sad Celebrations

The journey back was worse than the journey there. Jenna missed Alistair. The old man was her mentor and friend. There were many times along her travels where she wished to seek his advice. Once every so often, she would turn and she discovered he was not there. How her heart broke. She no longer had his presence. She mourned his loss and the loss of her companions Danyll and Kate. The sorrow of it all was almost too terrible to bear.

The army encountered very little resistance upon its return trip to Erenhil. The destruction throughout the countryside was evident. Most of the town and villages were deserted and laid in ruins. Lendaw was not as beautiful as Jenna once remembered it to be. It would take time to rebuild.

It would never be the same.

Jenna lamented over this last thought.

They travelled another quinti before they reached the outskirts of Erenhil. It was then that Jenna heard the singing:

> "Nai a ni, nai a ni, ta'am me o Delhailla.
> Don a crie.
> Nai a ni, nai a ni, sie a don'ea.
> Nai a ni, Nai a ni Vini, Nai a ni.

Nai a ni, nai a ni, ta'am me o Delhailla.
Don a crie.
Nai a ni, nai a ni, sie a don'ea.
Nai a ni, Nai a ni Vini, Nai a ni."

The words were different this time while the tune remained familiar. Confusion crossed Jenna's face. The tune was familiar. The words were not. Cryall sensed Jenna's perplexity. She rode alongside Jenna's horse. She leaned over and she softly whispered. The song you hear is the Sorrow Song. It is the plural version of the one I sang after Danyll's death.

The song was solemn and tranquil. As Jenna listen to the song, she began to get emotional. She wiped a tear from her eye before she managed to pull herself together.

The elves repeated the verse while the company marched slowly toward the castle's courtyard.

The party dismounted from their horses. They had arrived safely.

Maia, and her entourage, strode up to the armies, and greeted them saying, "Sal Tel Doe e Paevast; Welcome and peace."

Jenna busied herself with Gnoz care. The two talked as they started to unpack the horse. Jenna kept espying glances at Maia. She promptly turned away whenever Maia turned the attention back to Jenna.

Sensing that Jenna did not want a public scene, Maia only nodded to her in acknowledgment. Jenna was glad of her discretion.

Later that evening, Maia summoned Jenna to her quarters. Jenna, knowing she could no longer deter the Queen and she appeared as summoned. Upon entering the chamber, she discovered Donyld, Cryall and Cáel present as well.

Just as I thought. I could no longer delay their enquiries.

"Ah Jenna, please do take a seat and help yourself to anything you see spread out before you."

The table was full of different fruit and drink options. Jenna helped herself to some fruit and a drink. She sat down on the settee nearest to the window, she crossed her legs and she gave a sigh.

I am going to be here for a while, at least, until I have satisfied their questions.

"Comfy are you?" Maia paused. "Good, let us begin. We were wondering if you could describe the events of the last few pace-stays."

"Where would you like me to start," enquired Jenna?

"How about, where you and Alistair first confronted Anko and his men?"

Jenna reiterated all the events of the past few days. She described how she and Alistair heard a noise, how Alistair went on ahead to investigate, and how he confronted Anko, Donar and Kael. She continued to detail how Alistair managed to slay Kael and then confronted Anko and Donar. During a duel with Donar, Alistair's staff broke resulting in an explosion. Anko and Donar suffered injuries, but made their escape. Jenna recapitulated that she arrived and she discovered Alistair dying. She explained that before he died Alistair reacquired the Iluminar and he gave it to her.

She jumped forward to her confrontation with Donar. She explained that he too had a smaller piece of the Gentra and that attempted to use it against her. She described how she was losing the battle when the Iluminar responded, seemingly of its own accord. It flared to life destroying both crystals in the process. The explosive force killed Donar, knocked her down, and that she somehow survived.

Maia, Donyld, Cryall and Cáel became worried at the idea of the destruction of the crystals.

Jenna told of her journey into Anko's lair. She aired her concern that she no longer possessed the Iluminar, her fear of death and of her decision to trust Alistair, and to confront Anko regardless of the outcome. She stated how Anko overpowered her, how she was losing the battle, and the how situation appeared hopeless. She continued to explain that when it seemed the battle was over, a power stirred within her. She clarified that she finally understood that she was the Crux, that she held the ultimate answer against the Gentra and Anko, and that she was the living embodiment of the Iluminar.

She divulged how the power initial tiny grew to greater and greater until it became uncontainable at which point the power exploded. The magic obviated the Gentra and then Anko himself.

She concluded that she must have passed out. When she awoke, she discovered Cryall and Cáel were standing over her.

When Jenna finished, they were dumbstruck. Never in their wildest imagination could they have expected such a thing.

They were happy that Jenna succeeded and survived. There was much sorrow too. They were greatly saddened by lost a great friend, mentor and confidant. They had paid a great price for their success. They spent some time reminiscing about Alistair. They shared some laughter and they shared some tears.

After a while, Maia gave Jenna a hug and said, "You must be tired after your trip. Why not go to your room and you try to get some sleep? I believe we could all use some rest."

CHAPTER 32

Departures

Jenna spent most of her last days in Erenhil resting.

Her favorite pastime was playing Kinknox with Cáel for enjoyment. She noted to herself that her skill at the game was improving.

She may finally win a game.

She chuckled at the thought.

Early on the day of departure, Maia approached Jenna, "So, have you decided what you are going to do?"

Ever since Maia first posed this question, Jenna thought of nothing more. She found herself in a predicament. With Alistair's demise, she knew Lendaw required her services. She had inherent all of his responsibilities and duties. She understood the others hoped that she would take the reins.

She wanted to go home.

Jenna had a strong desire to return to Earth. Frankly, she was homesick. She hoped to return and to search for Matt and Dot. Though they were not her real parents, they were all she knew. They raised her, they loved her as their own child, and she realized that was what really mattered. With the immediate crisis over, she discovered she missed her parents and that she wished to see them again.

"I want to go back at least for a little while."

"I understand. Considering all you have been through, that is understandable. How long do you think you will be gone?"

"Not long, I no longer belong there. I am a different person. Besides, Cáel and I have decided to build a life together. I doubt that he would enjoy it there for long. I want to show him some of my world before we return."

"That is great news! Congratulations."

Jenna smiled, "Thanks."

The two women walked outside the castle grounds. They watched, as everyone prepared to leave.

Jenna realized that she was going miss this place. True, Lendaw was different from Earth. It had lots to offer. It was a simpler way of life from a bye-gone era. It was unpolluted and the air was fresh. On Lendaw, she would serve a higher purpose. She would be someone of service. It would offer her life meaning and she liked that idea.

Maia interrupted Jenna's thought, "We, Altmer, are remaining here. We are isolationists by nature. Now that the current crisis is over, we wish to remain apart. We will return to our old way of life and the tranquility that it brings. There has been too much excitement of late."

Maia hugged Jenna, "I will see you when you return." She left Jenna to her own. She wanted Jenna to have an opportunity to say her farewells to her friends.

The dwarves left the day before. Durkin and Bilpin gave their blessing to Jenna before they left. Jenna did not envy their work. They would be responsible for the rebuilding an entire race. All that they knew was gone. They would have to restart from scratch. A great undertaking she knew. She was confident in their skill. If any two people could do it, then it would be Durkin and Bilpin. She hugged them and they departed.

The Silvan, cousin to the Altmer, would be travelling with the Alyrans and then they would return to Lórien once they reached Alyra. Jenna did not know the Silvan well.

She briefly spoke with Caidor who invited her to visit Trillemara. He described that wonders of the forest, life from life. He wanted to show her the woods and to teach her of his people. Jenna agreed to visit the Silvan upon her returned to Lendaw. Caidor bowed slightly, made his excuses, and he departed.

Jenna went over to the Alyran encampment. She sought for Deskin and Gentwer. She found them with Dwendelmir where they were discussing old times and the events of the last few days. Jenna laughed and fretted as they described their many deeds and antics during the fighting. They were initially worried for Jenna as she went over the events of the past few cycles and they rejoiced at her success. They rejoiced that she was safe. Dwendelmir stated that he would be staying with the Altmer. The companions said their good-byes and then departed.

Jenna went to seek out Cáel and Donyld before she left. She let the cat out of the bag by telling Maia that Cáel and she would get married. They wanted to ask Donyld for permission before they proceeded with any marriage. She wasn't worried about his response. It was only a formality. It was customary to seek permission and she did not wish to break with that tradition.

Donyld was elated when he learnt the news that Jenna and Cáel would bond and he gave his blessing gladly. Jenna and Cáel told him of their plans to visit Earth. They explained that they would return once Jenna found her parents and she was certain of their safety.

Donyld told them that he had news of his own. He told them that with Maia's decision to remain with the Altmer, that Maia appointed Donyld as ruler of Alyra. He insisted that she erred and that she chose the wrong person.

Jenna and Cáel assured him that he would make a great king.

The next day, when only the elves remained, Cáel and Jenna bid farewell to Maia and the Altmer. She again assured them that she would return. Soon afterward, Jenna and Cáel left the shelter of Erenhil.

The trip to the Twin Mountains took seven days. They were in no hurry to reach their destination. Jenna wanted to absorb their surroundings before leaving Lendaw. When they finally reached the entry of the Portal of Ianua, Jenna turned to Cáel and she took his hand, "Well, my love, are you ready for the next adventure?"

The two lovers next stepped into the portal together and they were gone.

Edwards Brothers Malloy
Oxnard, CA USA
January 12, 2016